I0779147

Alpha & Omega

The Beginning …

Kevin D. Morris

MSE

MorningStar Enterprises / Publications

PUBLISHED BY

MORNINGSTAR ENTERPRISES / PUBLICATIONS

PHILADELPHIA, PENNSYLVANIA

This is a work of fiction. Apart from obvious historical or prophetic references to public figures, locales, and events, all human characters and incidents are the products of the author's imagination. Any actual or perceived similarities to anyone living or dead are purely coincidental.

All Scripture references are quoted from the King James Version (KJV) Bible.

To Brenda, *my wife*
for everything that you are to me
I love you!

To All My
Brothers and Sisters in Christ
Everywhere -
I treasure you all!

But above all
To *my* **Lord and Savior
Yeshua (Jesus), the
Christ** I thank, worship, and
adore **You**! Come quickly, **Lord**!

<u>Prologue</u>

"Hell from beneath is moved for thee to
meet thee at thy coming"
- Isaiah 14:9

He stood upon the highest pinnacle of the
Temple, the gaze of his piercing deep blue eyes
penetrating the cloud-filled expanse above. A
sinister smirk manifested as he changed his
focus from the heavens to the scene below
filled with the echoing din of multitudes.
Something was happening within him.
Something he had never experienced in all the
countless millennia that he had existed.
Something was being birthed in him, and even
though he, being an angel of light - the "Light
Bearer" in fact - sensed its covert darkness, yet
still he embraced it. As he scanned the masses
below consisting of roughly one-third of his
brethren, the embryonic darkness in his heart
fully manifested into Pride and Arrogance - and
Sin was born into the universe. Lucifer turned
his gaze heavenward again, and gave voice to
the evil now resident in his heart.

"I will ascend into heaven. I will exalt my throne above the stars of God: I will sit also upon the mount of the congregation, in the sides of the north: I will ascend above the heights of the clouds; I will be like the Most High." Barely had he finished uttering these words when suddenly two angels appeared, one on either side of him, brandishing golden swords that crackled with otherworldly energy.

"You are summoned!" spoke Michael fearlessly, and with great authority.

Lucifer began to smile, but it quickly turned into a sneer, as he realized that each of his fellow angelic defectors was also flanked by two loyal angels on either side of them as well. Lucifer nodded accedence, and in a moment, in the twinkling of an eye, a world filled with the angelic hosts was suddenly empty of them.

As Lucifer knelt before the Throne, he began to realize that he could no longer look directly into the glorious Light that emanated from the Throne. Though for eons prior to now, he had been able to walk up and down in the midst of the Throne and its Light, he now found himself literally unable to gaze into that same Light. As he pondered this, a voice as of many rushing waters emanated from the midst of the Throne.

"Lucifer, My son, darkness has birthed in your spirit. Therefore repent and return to Me, otherwise, sin lies at your door with eternal separation from Me as it's irrevocable payment and consequence. Choose life and live, for why will you die?"

"Master, I have chosen. I will ascend above the heights of the clouds; I will be like..."

"Satan, you shall be brought down to hell, to the sides of the pit", thundered the mighty voice from the midst of the Throne.

At that, there suddenly appeared a rift in the glassy sea-like floor of the Throne Room. In an instant, Lucifer, now called Satan, and all his fellow defectors, fell through the opening and out of Heaven. The Lord, sitting in the midst of the Throne, beheld as Satan fell like lightning towards the Earth. Down, down, down he plummeted, his angelic visage of perfect beauty transforming into one of a hideously deformed spirit of darkness. His rebellious cohorts also suffered the same fate as well, but some in addition were also chained and imprisoned in the Abyss - the Bottomless Pit. When Satan finally reached the Earth, he was so overwhelmed by what had just transpired that it took him a few seconds to realize the changes that had taken place in the Earth. Whereas his principality had before been a beautiful paradise, it too now bore the scars of divine judgment. The entire Earth had been laid waste and was void of any life whatsoever. Also missing were his subjects- his rebellious brethren - or so it seemed. At first, he didn't sense their presence, but then he heard them.

"Master, we are here," the voices said.

As Satan focused his eyes, he peered into the spiritual darkness and there he saw them - the former holy angels, now angels of darkness – demons, who were also hideously deformed like their now fallen prince. A smirk came across Satan's face as he now stared at the sky. He shook his fists toward Heaven, and declared, "I will yet ascend above the heights of the clouds." He then gathered his demons together and set about how to do just that.

Meanwhile, in Heaven, the LORD, seated in the midst of the Throne, spoke to the Lord and said, "Amen. It has begun."

Prologue II

> "To this end was I born, and for
> this cause came I into the world ..."
> *- John 19:37*

Michael stood at the ready, as did the rest of the heavenly hosts, with golden swords unsheathed - but there came forth no command from the Throne, as there had been no request from below. Michael, along with the rest of the angelic armies, stood perplexed and bewildered as they viewed the utterly horrific atrocity that was unfolding on the Earth below.

Michael realized that this was now the second time since he had been created that he was completely stupefied by an event that he neither understood nor comprehended. The first time was when the Lord divested Himself of His outward glory and wrapped Himself in human flesh, the flesh of those creatures He created and to whom He gave dominion over the Earth (who subsequently gave the dominion over to Satan). Now, these same rebellious creatures were in the process of crucifying the Lord of Hosts, the Creator - the very One who gives them life and sustains them.

Michael wondered within himself, "What is transpiring here? Why is the LORD allowing this to happen to the Lord? Why hasn't the Lord called for us? Why is there no command from the Throne to intervene?"

The response from the Throne to Michael, as well as to the rest of the heavenly hosts, was a calming, yet authoritative "Peace, be still".

Michael looked on, still at the ready, prepared to move in the blink of an eye. As he surveyed the scene below, his eyes caught a glimpse of a shadowy figure of darkness, moving in and out of the midst of the ignorant and unsuspecting hate-filled mob. Michael watched as Satan went about his evil work. Michael knew that whatever Satan was up to – ultimately, it would fail. Michael trusted in God and he knew that no matter how things may appear to be, the LORD God *is* God, and He reigns.

Chapter 1

"Men's hearts failing them for fear,
and for looking after those things
which are coming on the Earth:
for the powers of heaven shall be shaken.
- Luke 21:26

"Can you believe this" exclaimed the young man as he folded the newspaper to exhibit a particular story and handed it to his father. "I've heard a lot of crazy things in my line of work, but this is downright nuts", he continued as his father reread the story slowly to make sure he had read it right the first time. "How in the world can the courts find the homeowner liable for the injuries sustained by a burglar in the process of burglarizing said homeowner's home? Have they lost their minds?" queried Antwon Jackson, livid over what he had just read.

"Son, it's the world we live in now. There's no sense of right or wrong, no absolutes anymore. Everything is just…'relative', replied Will Jackson, turning to the sports section.

"Hey, I know it's early in the season, but the Eagles don't look too good, do they. They're 2-3."

"Great, Dad. I'm talking about injustice and you're talking sports" sighed Ant.

"Son, let me try to help put your mind at ease. It's going to get a whole lot worse before it gets better" assured Will.

"Never mind, Dad" said Ant quickly as he rolled his eyes to the ceiling. "I don't have time for a sermon. I've got to get to work. I just stopped by to see how you and mom were doing. When she awakes, tell her I was here and that I love her. Love you too, Pops" said Ant as gave his father a loving hug. "I'll stop by as soon as I get back from Israel".

"Be vigilant and take care of yourself over there" advised Will. "God be with you, son".

"Thanks, Dad, but it's a lot safer since Israel recently won the so-called 'War of Psalm 83' " replied Ant somewhat sheepishly. "I'm out".

"See ya" said Will, as Ant was closing the door behind him.

Will returned to the newspaper story that had disturbed his son. He began to think of all the chaos and injustice that existed in the world in general, and in the Middle East in particular.

He thought about how incredibly biased the nations and the world media had become against Israel, and nowhere was that more evident than at the United Nations. Resolution after resolution had been brought against Israel for the "atrocities" of defending itself from repeated attacks by her neighboring enemies, who had unashamedly continued their attacks even though "truces" were supposedly in place. Now, the entire world seemed to be against Israel ever since she nuked Damascus in retaliation for Syria firing missles armed with chemical gas agents into Israel during the Psalm 83 War. It seemed the whole world was "roaring" for Israel's destruction. If it were not for the United States with its one veto vote power, all the resolutions brought against Israel would have passed easily. And yet, though the whole world was aware of what was actually transpiring in the Middle East, not one single resolution had been brought against any of the terrorist nations that had attacked Israel.

"Truly, we live in perilous times, Lord", said Will as he put down the paper and headed to the bedroom to get dressed.

Dr. Greg Wersop couldn't stop trembling. He took a deep breath and made a concerted effort to do so just long enough to minutely recalibrate the coordinates for the observatory telescope. Finally successful in this attempt, Dr. Wersop nervously peered into the eyepiece yet again. His heart pounded and his pulse quickened as he made his way to the workstation monitors to peruse the data being streamed across the display. He couldn't believe his eyes. But he had to. Numbers don't lie. He sat down before he fell down.

For the past several years, as part of a coordinated effort in association with other observatories around the world, Dr. Wersop had been scanning the heavens for NEO (Near-Earth Objects). NEO are defined as asteroids, meteors, or comets that come within 28 million miles of Earth's orbit. In all the years of his searching, he had never found a single new NEO. Until now. Now he found **two**.

Dr. Wersop began to perspire profusely as his mind raced. He retrieved a cold bottled-water from the fridge as his mouth was becoming quite dry. After drinking half the bottle and composing himself as much as he could, he picked up the phone and called a friend at NASA.

"H-Hello, Tom? Hey, yeah it's me. No, I'm not alright. Tom, I found two. Yeah, two NEO, and Tom, …they're both headed right at us."

Chapter 2

" Therefore be ye also ready:
for in such an hour as you think not,
the Son of Man cometh."
- Matt. 24:44

First class. Finally. Antwon Jackson surveyed his surroundings in the luxury cabin of the DC797 jetliner that now taxied toward the runway for takeoff from Philadelphia International Airport. "So this is how the "other half" lives", he said to no one in particular. He smiled as he leaned back in the plush reclining seat. As he did so, a flight attendant approached him.

"Would you like anything to drink, sir?"

"A small glass of Romulan ale, please". He laughed within himself as a very puzzled look came over the flight attendant's face.

She replied, "I'm sorry sir, I don't know if we have that stocked on board today. Would you care for something else?"

Doing all that was in his power to keep from bustin' a gut, Ant (as he was called), with teary eyes and a grin as wide as the Cheshire Cat's, said, "I'll have a White Russian, please. Thank you".

She nodded, and as she walked away, he thought to himself, "Obviously, not a fellow Trekker". He smiled as his thoughts returned to that of his surroundings.

"Man oh man. They finally put me in 1st class. I guess winning a Pulitzer will do that for you"

Ant thought back over his relatively short life so far – the past failures, including both relationships and careers, about how it seemed that everything came to others with ease, and how anything positive only came to him after intense struggles, and those positives were few and very far between. He'd almost given up on a successful life until journalism saved him from certain oblivion. Now he was on his way to Jerusalem to cover the current peace initiatives. He had to wonder if it was truly worth the time and effort because, so far, each time no sooner had a truce been announced, one Islamic faction or another would break said truce and attack Israel. Heck, he thought, they can't even seem to get along with each other, much less the Israelis, who were having their own internal problems as well. Their government leadership was weak and failing to act in the best interests of the nation. Ant sighed as he contemplated the minefield that was his current assignment.

"Well, it's going to be a long flight to Tel Aviv. Might as well get comfortable."

Ant reclined as far back as the luxury seat would allow and relaxed. As he did so, he overheard a conversation between the nearby flight attendants.

"He requested what?"

"Romulan ale. I told him that we didn't have any in stock. We don't, do we?"

Ant let out a quiet little laugh, grinning and showing all 32. He then stared out the nearby window as the DC797 quietly rose to the starlit heavens.

Although Joseph Levinson was standing outside the office of the Israeli Prime Minister, his mind, at least for this moment, was in another place entirely. It seemed he couldn't stop thinking about her. He had only met her a few months ago, having been introduced by his sister, Sarah. Yes, she was definitely on his mind, and it seemed that Miriam Reubens was there to stay.

"They're about to begin", alerted an observant aide.

With that, Joey came back to his present location completely and strode assuredly into the Prime Minister's office. Although this wasn't the first time that Joey had been in the PM's office - in fact, in his position as Israeli Liaison to the White House, he'd entered this room many times before - this was the first time that he felt an air of uncertainty and quiet desperation from his colleagues assembled therein. Without question, the subject before them now – how to deal with the angry nations of the world since winning the Psalm 83 War and finally bringing a lasting peace to Israel. Tensions had been escalating higher and higher in recent weeks. All were hopeful that during the current truce, due to the overwhelming victory of the recent war, a real and lasting peace could be hammered out.

As Joey reflected on these things, the PM began to speak.

"I have received a request from the Secretary-General of the United Nations to attend a peace summit in Brussels next month. I have accepted his invitation. This summit will again be moderated by the Quartet.

Everyone assented agreement and set about how to best bring a peace accord into being. As everyone filed out of the PM's office, most feeling a little more upbeat than when they had entered, Joey wondered why it was that he had the strangest feeling that his people were about to place themselves in the greatest peril that they had ever known. He shook himself. "Come on, Joey. Get it together now. What, are you some kind of psychic now? What do you know?"

He laughed nervously to himself as his mind turned back to warm thoughts of Miriam. As he walked out into the cool September night, he touched his Bluetooth headset and said, "Miriam". Immediately, the automatic voice-dialer feature went to work as Joey strode towards his car in the parking garage.

"Hi, Miriam. Joey. How are you? Fine. Listen, I'm thinking of catching a movie tomorrow night and I was wondering if you would like to go with me. Great! I'll pick you up around 7 o'clock and then we'll…". His voice trailed off as he slid into his Lexus LS430, put it in gear, and then drove off toward home.

The wind chimes created a melodious sound as the front door was opened, and nearly duplicated it as the door was closed.

"Hi, honey. I'll be right down", came the equally sweet (to him anyway) voice of his wife of 30 years.

"Take your time, baby. I'm not goin' anywhere," replied Will as he plopped down into his favorite chair. As he leaned back in the recliner, he grabbed the remote and turned the A/V system on. "Let's see what's goin' on in the world today" he said as he tuned in UNN (United News Network).

"Hello handsome", purred Ruby Jackson as she sat on his lap and gave him a long loving kiss. "How did the street witnessing go today?" she lovingly intoned as she caressed his face with warm kisses from her soft lips.

"It was awesome" replied Will. "The Lord really moved today. His presence was truly manifested, and on top of all that, seven souls were added to the Kingdom. I'm very glad that I pressed my way to do street witnessing today, although I'm still perplexed as to why the car battery would just up and die like that, especially since we purchased it only a few short months ago. Hmm...seems like someone is up to his old tricks. The adversary is doing whatever he can to try to stop us because he knows that his time is very short. However, the Word of God promises that nothing that he brings against us will prosper. Hallelujah!!! Praise the Lord!!!"

"My, my. We really did enjoy ourselves today" said Ruby as she slowly began to rise.

"The day is not over yet, darling" he half-whispered as he pulled her back into his arms.

"Will, I have to get dinner on the table" she said in mock protest, all the while melting into his warm embrace.

"Baby, now you know the Word of God says that man cannot live by bread alone" he replied, and they both shared a tender, love-filled laugh as they both arose and proceeded to the dining room. Just as they reached the dinner table, the phone rang.

"I'll get it", said Will. "Hello? Antwon? Hi son, how are you? Good. Good. How was your flight? Oh…I'm sure they found you amusing as well. Well, listen, if you need anything, don't hesitate to call. Okay, I'll give her your love. Take care and be watchful. I love you too, son. Bye".

"Hon, Antwon sends his love and says his plane has landed safely in Tel Aviv. He'll be on his way to Jerusalem in about half an hour".

"Will, I'm concerned about Ant being over there, especially with all the tension going on right now", said Ruby, expressing her fears.

"Honey, I wouldn't worry too much. Antwon is a grown man and he can take care of himself. Besides, we'll continually lift him before the Lord and ask the Lord to keep, guide, and protect him. He'll be okay. Oh, by the way, I learned something extremely interesting today. You know how Yeshua said that 'no man knows the day or the hour' of His return for the Church? Well, get this, that phrase was a Jewish idiom that referenced Rosh

Hashanah, which was celebrated over two days because no one was certain which day or at which hour the new moon would appear, so to speak. It's just possible that Yeshua was actually giving us a hint as to the "time" of His return. Check the calendar. Rosh Hashanah started yesterday at sundown. Who knows?!"

Ruby smiled as they both sat at the table and began to give the Lord thanks for their meal and make supplication for their son.

Ant had no sooner stepped into the shower in his room at the King David Hotel when his phone began ringing.

"It figures", he huffed as he headed to answer. "Yes?" he snorted into the phone. "Oh, Joey! Dude, how ya doin'. No, it's not a bad time, not at all. I was just about to take a shower, that's all. It's cool. I was going to call you at your office, but I see that ya tracked me down first. So, when and where, buddy? Ok, sounds like a plan to me. I'll see you later. 'Bye now".

Ant smiled as he hung up the phone and returned to the shower. He thought how good it would be to see his old college pal after so many years, and even though it was official business that brought their circles together again, he was looking forward to hanging with Joey in the "City of Peace".
"Hmm....City of Peace. What a strange moniker for a place that forever seems to be the center of strife and violence" he mused to himself.
"Well, I, for one, plan to have a good time while I'm here. I'm gonna get my party on and spend some time checking out the club scene with my pal Joey", he said to himself as he turned the knob and a welcome spray of hot water cascaded over and down his body.

Haziel and Arizael stood unnoticeable in the midst of Ant's hotel room.

"Our charges shall meet soon. We must be watchful, for the Evil One desires to kill them both, but the Lord has destined otherwise", said Arizael.

With that being said, Haziel vanished from the scene as Arizael went and stood guard next to Ant, brandishing his golden sword, alert and at the ready. Ant, completely oblivious to Arizael's presence, was into the 2nd chorus of *his* rendition of Stevie Wonder's "Livin' For The City", much to Arizael's "delight".

All of Heaven was abuzz with adoration and excited expectation. Everyone sensed that the "time" was close at hand when the LORD would send His Son back to Earth to retrieve His Bride, the Church. The moment that they were joyously anticipating finally came. The LORD, seated in the midst of the throne, spoke to His Son seated at His right-hand, saying "Lord, it's time. Go receive your Bride. Michael and Gabriel will accompany you". At that command, the Lord Yeshua (Jesus) arose from His Father's throne and vanished from sight, along with Michael and Gabriel, only to reappear a moment later descending into Earth's extreme upper stratosphere. Suddenly and simultaneously, the Lord Yeshua gave a great shout – **"Come up here"**, as Gabriel blasted the Lord's golden shofar the last of three times, and Michael gave a great battle cry with which to assemble the angelic hosts of Heaven.

Will Jackson lay wide-awake in bed during the pre-dawn hours contemplating his relationship with his son, Antwon. Most predominate in his thoughts was how he had allowed their recently-ended estrangement to prevent him from sharing his and his wife's fairly new-found faith in Jesus Christ for the past three years. He never had the opportunity he desired to truly share and expound the gospel with Antwon the way his heart longed to do. He determined that the very next time he saw Antwon, he would say more than "You need Jesus in your life". Will also was worried about time. He knew they were running out of it. Will had become an ardent student of biblical prophecy and he recognized all the signs of the end-time as they were occurring daily throughout the world – the worldwide rejection of Christ and Judeo-Christian ethics and morals, a planet in travail - manifesting in monster earthquakes, tsunamis, hurricanes, tornados, flash floods, wildfires; a global push towards a one-world government with a global currency, a global military, and a global ruler. As troubling as these signs were, there were two other signs that pointed to the time in which he lived even more so. Christ said that at the time of His return, it would be as the days of Sodom and Gomorrah, and as the days of Noah. The days of Sodom and Gomorrah refers to the widespread activity and acceptance of homosexuality, while the days of Noah refers to everyone doing what was right in their own eyes – meaning people were doing whatever they wanted to do regardless of any laws, rules, or authority whatsoever. No matter how big or small the transgression, people were doing whatever came into their hearts to do – from committing mass murder to running red lights at abandon, people were "doing what was right in their own eyes". Will quietly prayed for Antwon's salvation.

Ruby, somehow sensing her husband's insomnia, awoke out of her sleep.

"Honey, you alright? What's the matter?"

"Just thinkin' 'bout Ant, that's all. I wish I had shared the gospel with him. Well, I'm gonna take care of that as soon as I see him again."

"I'm sure you will hon", replied Ruby as she arose out of bed to go to the bathroom.

"Babe, would you care for some breakfast? "asked Will as he climbed out of bed also.

"Yes, that would be wonderful, sweetie," replied Ruby as she donned her robe.

"Okay baby, you got it!" he smilingly half-whispered to his adoring wife.

Suddenly, their attention was drawn heavenward as they both heard what sounded like loud trumpet blasts. Will then stared at his wife. She, as well as he, had been transformed in a moment, in the twinkling of an eye, into a young, radiantly glowing being. They both looked toward the heavens as they heard a great shout:

"Come up here".

They both began to rise up, passing right

through the ceiling and roof. As they passed beyond the roof, they saw multitudes of beings like themselves also rising through the air. Accelerating more and more each second as they soared through the atmosphere, they saw a bright Light at the apex of the cloud-filled expanse. The closer they approached the bright Light, the more it seemed to coalesce into the form of a Being quite like themselves, only greater. Also, the closer they got to this Person, the more their entire being resonated with life, power and joy. They knew, of course, that this was none other than their Lord and Savior, Yeshua, the Christ, Son of the Most High God, come for His Body, the true Church, to take her home to His Father's House.

Chapter 3

> "Come, my people, enter
> thou into thy chambers, and shut thy doors about thee:
> hide thyself as it were for a little moment,
> until the indignation be overpast.
> *– Isaiah 26:20*

Ant, groggy with sleep, buried his head under the pillows, trying desperately to drown out the loud commotion in the hotel hallway.

"What is wrong with these people? Don't they know they're supposed to be quiet in the hallways? *Some* people just might be tryin' to sleep," he murmured to himself.

Just as he managed to get comfortable again, the phone began to ring incessantly.

"I *don't* believe this", Ant groaned as he fumbled for the phone. "Hello?" fumed Ant, clearly irritated at this latest interruption of his rest.

"Ant. Thank God, you're there."

"Joey? Hey man, what's wrong?" intoned Ant, suddenly alert and sitting up in the bed.

"Turn on the TV, man. Oh my God. It's

incredible. I…I don't know what's going on."

Ant grabbed the remote, turned on the TV, and sat in stunned silence as various scenes of worldwide panic and devastation paraded before his eyes on the screen. Reports of terrible accidents occurring all over the world: trains derailing, suddenly pilotless planes falling out of the sky, innumerable car wrecks involving thousands of driverless cars, and hundreds of thousands, perhaps millions, reported missing. There were even some obviously delirious reports of people vanishing right before people's eyes.

"What the hell…? Joey, what in God's name is goin' on? Does anybody know what happened?" he asked in a very low, nervous voice.

"No. No one has a clue as to what actually happened. All we can gather is that whatever has happened, it seems to have occurred globally and simultaneously" replied Joey with a slight hint of fear in his voice.

"Globally *and* simultaneously?" repeated Ant incredulously. "What in God's name could do that?" he inquired of his friend, not really expecting a satisfying answer from him. Joey did not disappoint.

"I haven't the foggiest", replied Joey. "Listen, Ant. I'm heading over to the PM's office. Why don't you join me over there. I'll leave your name at the front gate so they'll be expecting you. That way you'll be able to get access into the building. I'll meet you in the lobby and we'll go from there directly to see the Prime Minister."

"O.K., I'm on my way. See you soon. Bye." replied Ant as he was quickly getting out of bed. He hung up the phone and began getting dressed, listening intently to the various reports coming from the TV. It was unbelievable. Hospitals and homes worldwide were reporting nurseries missing all their newborn babies, toddlers, and little children. In many places, entire families were reported missing, while in other cases, only one or two family members were missing, but still yet, in most families, there wasn't anyone missing at all.

"I don't get it. I just don't get it. What in the world is happening?" Ant wondered aloud to himself.

Having quickly finished dressing, he grabbed his room's keycard, hurried downstairs, jumped into a cab, and sped off toward the PM's office.

Sarah Levinson and Miriam Reubens were both terrified and near tears. Their waiter, who just a second ago stood before them bearing their orders, had suddenly vanished into thin air, causing their plates to crash to the floor. Also, a couple at a nearby table had disappeared as well; their clothes and jewelry being left behind.

"What's h-happening. Is this some type of t-t-terrorist attack?" asked a quite shaken Miriam.

"I - I don't know" replied an equally frightened Sarah.

"W-What do we do? Should we run or keep still?" inquired Miriam nervously.

"Run to where? We don't know what's going on. Let's stay where we are. I'm going to try to call Joey," said Sarah, as she pulled her cell phone out of her purse and began to dial. A voice promptly informed her that all circuits were busy due to unusually heavy usage. "All the circuits are busy. I'll try again in a few minutes. Let's head back to my place in the meantime, okay?" offered Sarah as she began to gather her things.

"Okay" replied Miriam, rising from the table as she grabbed her pocketbook, quickly joining Sarah as they made their way out of the restaurant and headed for the car. It wasn't until they were outside that they began to realize the scope of the terror that they had encountered inside. There were a few car accidents, screams of people vanishing, and parents hysterically searching for their little children. "What in God's name is going on?" said Sarah as she surveyed the scene before them.

It was more than she could bear.

"Let's go", she yelled over the din to Miriam.

The two ran to the car, got in, and took off - Sarah putting the Jaguar X-type through its paces. Normally, at the speed at which she was maneuvering through the city streets, she would have easily received a speeding ticket. However, at the moment, the police had much more pressing matters on their hands.

Satan was enraged. Not only had his "domain" been invaded by the Enemy, but also those who were once under his attack, now glorified and looking like the Enemy, were snatched away in a moment. He didn't even have time to try to hinder them, so quickly were they raptured away. Satan immediately garnered all his minions to pursue the Body of Christ. Immediately, they were met by all the holy angels in the midst of the heavens, and there was war in heaven with Michael and his angels fighting against Satan and his demons. The archangel Michael and his holy angels easily overwhelmed and defeated Satan and his army of demons, who found themselves cast down to the surface of the Earth. Satan turned his gaze skyward and ventured to fly there, but found that he could not. He attempted to do so again, and again he was not able to do so. Satan was uncontrollably furious. He knew now that his time was extremely short.

"Well, now that the "salt" and "light" has

been removed, nothing now restrains me from putting *my* program into full effect", fumed Satan as he stood upon an altar built for worship to him. It was erected in the secret chambers of the castle owned and inhabited by the newest and most highly adored prince in the Middle East - Prince Faakhir Abdul-Waahid.

Will Jackson stood in awe. Even in his glorified state, possessing perfect knowledge, knowing even as he is known, he was in complete and utter awe. He stood among millions, yet they were one. One Body. As one with perfect knowledge, he knew that they were standing before the Judgment Seat of Christ. As he looked around, he could see that they were located just outside the City - the New Jerusalem. The City was humongous. It shimmered, glowed, and radiated with the glory of its Designer and Builder. Will's attention returned to the scene just before him, for the Lord had begun judging His people - His Body. This was a very somber moment - if a moment can be measured in eternity - but a moment was all it took, for the Lord judged every single person, individually, at the same "moment". Will found himself the recipient of quite a few crowns - most of them unexpected! However, he, as most everyone around him, felt shame for the instances of selfishness and unfaithfulness revealed to him by the Lord. Everyone wept.

As the Lord Yeshua personally wiped away every tear, Will, along with the rest of the Body, heard Him say, gesturing towards the City, "Come, you blessed of My Father: enter into the joy of your Lord". Immediately, they were in the glorious City, standing before the throne of God the Father. Yeshua stood with His Bride, and presented her - individually - all in one "moment" to the Father. The Father blessed the union of His Son and His Bride. Then all of Heaven rejoiced, and Yeshua began to sing and dance with joy amongst His Bride. Will's entire being resonated with joy unspeakable. As Yeshua finished His dance, He returned to His Father's throne and resumed His seat at the Father's right hand. As He did so, voices, lightnings, and thunderings proceeded from out of the throne, and the four living creatures in the midst of and around the throne continuously gave glory to Him that sat on the throne, saying, "Holy, holy, holy, Lord God Almighty, which was, and is, and is to come".

At this, all the Redeemed, as one, fell prostrate and cast their crowns of gold before the throne, saying, "You are worthy, O Lord, to receive glory and honor and power: for you have created all things, and for your pleasure they are and were created".

As they stood upon their feet again, an angel declared, "Blessed are they which are called unto the marriage supper of the Lamb". Immediately, everyone was in what appeared to be a heavenly banquet hall that seemed to stretch beyond measure. Will was taking in the beauty of the setting, when he heard his new name being called by a sweet, melodious voice that seemed somewhat familiar to him.

"Hello handsome", a beaming and gloriously radiant Ruby smiled to her co-Bride / former husband.

"Hello gorgeous" he replied, with more love than he ever thought possible. "Join me for dinner?"

"Absolutely, but I seem to remember someone saying something about man not living by bread alone or something like that", she lovingly jested.

They both shared a heartfelt laugh as they joined hands and headed to their seats at the banquet table, reuniting with family and greeting friends, old and new.

———————————————

Ant arrived at the gate just minutes after Joey had entered. As he approached the gate, one of the guards, obviously expecting him, asked if he was Mr. Jackson and requested to see his I.D. The guard checked the photo I.D. against the photo and information they *already* had on Antwon. Assured that Antwon's I.D.

was legitimate, he then proceeded to check out Antwon. After a very thorough search, Antwon was allowed to pass through the gate and was directed to the lobby where Joey awaited his arrival. At long last, he saw his ol' college bud, standing just a short distance away, hanging up his cell phone.

"Joey!", Ant half-shouted as he hurried to greet his friend.

"Ant! Man, it's great to see you! How have you been?

"Fine, fine. That is 'til now. Joey, what in God's name is going on? It seems like the world is just losin' it."

"I'm afraid it gets a little worse by the minute. Ant, I just got off the phone with my liaison office. It would seem that your government has been adversely effected by this phenomenon. Some of your members of Congress, and some state governors, as well as many other state and local officials have "vanished" and cannot be accounted for. Your country, needless to say, is in crisis and on the highest level of alert status."

"Damn!" replied Ant in mild shock, "this is a total nightmare".

"Indeed it is. Let's get to the PM's office

and see if they've received any more intelligence on what's happening".

"Lead the way. I'm right behind you", replied Ant, as the two men hurried down the hallway to the elevators.

As the two men neared the entrance to the PM's office, they could see and hear a flurry of activity. Upon entering, Joey was immediately asked to join the officials at the table. Joey complied and showed Ant to a chair directly behind him. The PM called the group to order.

"Gentlemen. We are all somewhat aware of the phenomenon that has occurred this day. While we do not as yet know exactly what has transpired, we do know that it has left our world in a state of chaos. As such is the case, I have put our armed forces on the highest alert status as a precaution, in the event that our enemies would try to use the current situation as a opportune moment to attempt a sneak attack against our nation. Our only ally, the United States, is itself, in a state of crisis of its own, with much of its government missing. However, I'm afraid that's not all that is missing. It would appear that quite a vast number of their populace has also "vanished into thin air", so to speak, and as if that were not troubling enough," said the PM as he made eye contact with everyone seated at the table," according to the latest intel that we've been able to gather, those that have gone missing were some of our staunchest supporters and, it would seem that most, if not all, were so-called *'born-again' Christians*".

At those words, the room became abuzz again, and the hairs on the back of Ant's neck stood up. "My parents!" exclaimed Ant in a whisper. "Oh God, Joey! I have to check on my parents! Where's a phone I can use?"

"Right over there, Ant! What's up?"

"My parents! They're totally into that Jesus thing!"

"Oh, Ant! I had no idea. When did this happen?"

"A few years ago. I haven't really talked to them about it, though. They seem to be happy with it, so it's okay for them".

"And you?"

"Well, honestly, I really don't know much about it other than being told 'You need Jesus in your life' by my ol' man. Right now, after hearing what your PM just said, all I want to do is make sure that my parents are safe".

"Sure, sure. I can understand that. Here. Dial 9 to get an outside line. I hope everything is okay with your parents".

Ant pressed as quickly as he could the fourteen numbers required to reach his parent's home, however, all that he heard was that volume was extraordinarily heavy and that all circuits were busy and to please try his call again later.

"Damn!" exclaimed Ant, slumping into a nearby chair.

"What? What's wrong?" inquired Joey, somewhat alarmed.

"The lines. They're all tied up. I can't get through right now. I'll have to try a little later. Damn!"

"Try to calm down. I'm sure you'll get through to them pretty soon. In the meantime, let's try to figure out just what the hell is going on. There must be some answers somewhere. We just need to keep on looking until we find them. Alright?"

"Sounds good to me. A team again, just like back in the good ol' days. Only now, it's much more serious, and that's understating it!"

Just then, an official burst into the room, picked up a remote, pressed a few buttons, simultaneously lowering a huge flat-panel monitor and announcing to the PM and all in attendance, "Everyone, your attention, please", as he pointed to the screen, now filled with live footage from UNN. There was an audible gasp from the onlookers as the screen was filled with violence of every sort; being committed in all parts of the world, and covered live by UNN. Anarchy reigned supreme and men were doing whatever their hearts desired to do: murder, rape, robbery, and all types of perversion. Nothing was restrained.

"Joey, what the hell *is* this?" asked Ant, staring at the screen in disbelief.

"Hell, it would seem, is exactly what this is," replied Joey, "and it appears that the whole world has gone there in a hand-basket".

<u>Chapter 4</u>

> "I am come in My Father's name,
> and ye receive Me not:
> if another shall come in his own name,
> him ye will receive."- *John 5:43*

Sarah and Miriam huddled together in Sarah's den, being careful not to go near any windows. Still frightened nearly out of their wits, they attempted to calm one another. It began to work. Feeling a little bit better, Sarah tried to reach Joey for the umpteenth time. Expecting to hear the "all circuits busy" message again, she was somewhat surprised to hear ringing at the other end.

"Hello?"

"Joey!"

"Sarah? Thank God! Are you okay?"

"Yes, yes, I'm fine. Miriam is here with me, and other than being scared out of our wits, we're okay. Joey, I know this is going to sound like I've lost my mind, but you have to believe me..."

"Sarah, it's okay. It's happened *everywhere*. I can believe anything you tell me, sis. Ant's here and we're going to try to find out exactly what happened today."

"Joey, we're so scared. What should we do?"

"First of all, calm yourselves. I don't think that whatever it was that happened...well, I think it's over. Just be very cautious about people around you. It seems like almost everyone has just about lost their minds. Where are you?"

"Home. Hiding down in the den."

"Okay. Make sure all the doors and windows are locked and secure, then return to the den. Ant and I will be there shortly. Don't answer the doorbell. I'll use my spare key. We'll let ourselves in, and we'll holler down to you before coming down to the den."

"Alright. Please hurry, Joey. We're so scared."

"Just sit tight, sis. We're on our way. Shalom."

Shadows played on the walls of the cavernous dark room, caused by the light coming from the flickering flames of the torches aligned along the walls. A dark-robed figure emerged from the shadows and knelt before a stone altar that featured an upside-down crucifix.

"Oh, how I hate the Nazarene" he hissed, "and His followers with their sanctimonious, holier-than-thou love and compassion. They are so weak; they make me want to vomit! I hate them so! They don't seem to understand, that it is through strength and power that one rules. I would truly have taught them that hard lesson, were they still here, but being the cowards they are, they have deserted the masses to be with Him. I loathe them, and I loathe Him even more!"

A putrid odor suddenly filled the room, accompanied by an overbearing sense of the presence of absolute evil, as Satan manifested himself upon the stone altar.

"Your heart is one after my own, my child", pronounced the dark and powerful ruler of this world-system. "Therefore have I chosen you to be my son. I will give you all the kingdoms of this world to rule, if you will continue to worship me and give yourself to me completely - mind, body, and ...soul. What say you?"

Prince Faakhir gazed into the eyes of the tempter, bowed before him, and replied, "I accept, my lord. Thy will be done".

At that, Satan laid his "hands" upon the man's head and said, "I am Anti-god, the Devil. You are Antichrist, the Beast. Arise, my son, for our time has come".

Will, Ruby, and the rest of the Body of Christ stood before the throne of God the Father, who held a book sealed with seven seals in His right hand. A mighty angel loudly proclaimed, "Who is worthy to open the book, and to loose the seals thereof?"

"I AM", replied the Lord Yeshua, the

Lamb of God, as He took the book out of the right hand of God the Father. As He did so, His Bride fell prostrate before Him, and sang a new song, saying "Thou art worthy to take the book, and to open the seals thereof: for thou wast slain, and hast redeemed us to God by thy blood out of every kindred, and tongue, and people, and nation; and hast made us unto our God kings and priests: and we shall reign on the earth".

Then all of the heavenly hosts joined in with a loud voice saying, "Worthy is the Lamb that was slain to receive power, and riches, and wisdom, and strength, and honor, and glory, and blessing".

After this, every created creature, whether they be in Heaven, on the earth, in Hell, or in the seas, was heard to say, "Blessing, and honor, and glory, and power, be unto Him that sits upon the throne, and unto the Lamb for ever and ever".

And the four living creatures said "Amen", whereupon the Bride of Christ again joyously fell prostrate and worshiped Him that liveth for ever and ever.
The Lord Yeshua then, having taken the book, opened the first seal.

Ant, Joey, Sarah, and Miriam sat huddled around the TV monitor located in Sarah's nicely furnished den. Accounts of the day's events were being aired on almost every channel.

"No one seems to know what happened! "exclaimed Miriam, as she pulled a light blanket around her shoulders, more out of fear than for being a little chilled.

"Look at it. The world's in utter chaos", said Ant.

Suddenly, a "Special Report" began to be broadcast.

"It has just been learned by UNN that, in reaction to today's devastating events, the world's financial markets, already teetering on the brink, have crashed completely. Billions upon billions in world currency have been lost. Precious metals, like gold, silver, and platinum, have also lost their value. We are also beginning to receive reports of large numbers of suicides occurring around the world, especially in the financial districts. The United Nations is in emergency session to try to cope with and resolve the disastrous events and issues of the day. Stay tuned to UNN as we will continue to bring you live coverage of these events", announced the somewhat stunned anchorperson.

"Oh…my…God!" whispered Ant. "This can't be happenin', it just can't be happenin', man.

"Quick. Come on, let's go", exclaimed Joey as he hurriedly headed for the front door.

"Where we goin'?, asked Ant, as he and the women rushed to catch up.

"To the market down the street. If we hurry, we may still be able to buy food and supplies. We'll need to stock up as much as we can. No telling when, how, or even if we'll be able to buy them later. Oh, and Ant, you should check out of your hotel room. You're staying with me, dude".

"Alright, I'll do that after we're done at the market".

"By the way, have you contacted your folks yet?"

"Not yet. I hope they're okay. I'll try

again later".

"Try not to worry, dude. Okay people, let's go".

The prince of darkness was concluding a meeting of his princes and highest ranking generals.

"...so therefore, this is what I command you to do. In the past, we have conspired to put every man against his neighbor, especially in the case of heads of state. What I will now is that you cause men to accept the terms of the peace treaty that my son is about to present to the world. Also, move the people to exalt my son, and to adore him, and you, yourselves, are to aid and abet him whenever and wherever he has need of you. My will be done", hissed Satan.

At that, a myriad of demons vanished, returning to their worldwide seats of power and influence to hand down the orders to those under their command.

Although in actuality it had only been slightly more than two weeks since the "disappearances", it felt more like two years, especially for Ant. He still had not been able to get in contact with his parents, and he was beginning to feel panicky.

"Listen, said Joey, the governments have resumed air travel as of yesterday. Catch a flight back and check on your folks, then call us and let us know how the situation stands."

"I guess you're right. I'll go nuts over here not knowing how they are or even *if* they are."

"If you don't mind, Antwon, I'd like to go along with you", said Sarah.

"Sure, that'll be great! I can use all the moral support I can get right now. Thank you, Sarah."

"Don't mention it. I could use a little diversion right about now."

The Beast looked out over the assembled dignitaries representing every nation on the face of the earth. The President of the UN Security Council was addressing the General Assembly.

"…the horrific calamity that has beset our world, and so in closing, let it be known to you that we, the UN Security Council, highly and strongly make recommendation to the General Assembly, that they both confirm Prince Faakhir Abdul-Waahid as the new Secretary-General and also grant emergency powers to the Secretary-General, enabling him to adequately address the current tragedy and other issues worldwide that are threatening to tear our world apart. We also, in light of the spectacular leadership demonstrated by Prince

Faakhir, do highly and strongly recommend that he be appointed as Secretary-General for life."

At this pronouncement, the entire General Assembly stood and gave a thundering 3-minute ovation. When everyone had resumed their seat, they proceeded to vote unanimously to approve all the recommendations of the Security Council. Afterwards, the President of the Security Council presented the Secretary-General to the assembly.

"Ladies and gentleman, I give you, the first-ever Chancellor of the World Union - Prince Faakhir Abdul-Waahid."

The assembly jumped to their feet yet again, this time for a full six minutes with an ovation that was nearly deafening. As the Beast stood before the podium, taking in the adoration and, yes, even the worship that was being given him, a sinister smile crept across his face. In his own country he was a prince among his people, but now, he was the de facto ruler of the world!

"Yes. Worship me. Let all the earth adore me", he thought to himself as the ovation continued. "Worship your lord and master!"

———————————

Ant and Sarah pulled into his parents' driveway and parked behind the dark green Camry LE sitting spotlessly before them. A good sign, thought Ant, until he saw the number of newspapers piled in a heap before the front door.

"Not a good sign" he half-murmured to himself before pulling out his copy of the spare key to the house.

"Hellooo", he said loudly as they entered the house." Anybody home? Hellooo. Mom? Dad? ".

Silence.

"I'll check down here, you go check upstairs," said Sarah.

"Alright" replied Ant as he headed for the staircase, all the while calling out for his parents.

Sarah walked into the dining room, and on through to the kitchen, noticing that everything was immaculately kept, with nothing seemingly out of place. She had just finished checking the library and was about to check out the den when she heard a loud groan come from the floor above. She hurried upstairs to find Ant in the master bedroom, on his knees, in the midst of two piles of bedroom clothes with a wedding band atop each pile.

"Oh no. Oh Ant, I'm so sorry" said Sarah as she began to weep.

"Why? Why God? I just wanna know why," sobbed Ant as the tears began to flow uncontrollably.

Sarah knelt and embraced him and tried to console and comfort him as best she could. Ant gratefully accepted Sarah's comforting arms and laid his heavy-hearted soul on her shoulder and wept for nearly half an hour.

Joey and Miriam glanced at each other

nervously as they watched UNN's special report covering the official inauguration of Prince Faakhir Abdul-Waahid as Chancellor of the World Union. Miriam jumped as the phone rang.

"I got it", said Joey, leaping out of his chair. "Hello?"

"Hey Joey, it's me, Ant."

Joey could tell right away by the sound of Ant's voice that things weren't okay at all, and he knew why.

"Oh man, Ant. I am so sorry. Is there anything that you need for me to do? Just name it, and it's done."

"No. No, there's nothing that anyone can do to change this. I just have to accept the fact that my folks are gone."

"I don't know what to say, Ant. I'm at a complete loss for words. I just feel so helpless."

"I know, man, and I appreciate your desire to help. Thanks."

"You are most welcome, brother. So, what are you going to do now? Are you guys heading back tonight?"

"Well, we decided to stay stateside for a few days before heading back. Say, what do you guys think of this "Chancellor of the World

Union" business? Can you believe it"!

"Yeah, did you see that? Personally, I don't care for it much. 'Absolute power corrupts absolutely', remember?"

"Yeah, I hear ya. Well, I'll call you guys tomorrow. Sarah is popping some popcorn as we speak. She says hello. We're going to see if we can find a decent movie to watch. My folks...my folks have a collection of DVDs here", Ant finally managed to say.

Joey heard the choking in Ant's voice and his heart ached for his friend.

"Okay, Ant. Take care of yourself and Sarah. Give her my love. Our hearts are with you. Talk to you tomorrow. Shalom."

Joey could barely relate what had happened, to Miriam, before he had to sit down. The tears flowed for his friend.

Early the next morning at 6 am, the

phone awakened Joey.

"Hello?" he spoke groggily into the receiver before realizing he had the wrong end, and turning it around, repeated "Hello?" into the transmitter.

"Joey! It's me, Ant. Man, have we got something to show you guys. We're catching the next available plane back. See you guys tonight. Gotta go! Our flight is boarding. Peace."
Click. Dial tone.

"Wha-at?" puzzled Joey, half awaking out of sleep, still not quite sure whether he was dreaming this or not. Barely managing to hang up, he turned over and went back to sleep.

Elijah and Moses stood before the throne of God as He gave them their assignment. After the Lord Yeshua finished speaking, they replied with one voice "Your will be done, O

Lord." At that, the two vanished from before the throne and a moment later appeared on the Temple Mount in Jerusalem.

As surprising as their sudden manisfestation on the Temple Mount was, even more startling was their *visual appearance*. Their robes were gleaming white and although they possessed mortal bodies, they still nonetheless shined from spending millenia in the presence of God Almighty.

"Hear, O Israel: The LORD our God is one LORD" thundered Elijah in a voice that carried for miles around.

"Lift up your heads, O ye gates; even lift up, ye everlasting doors; and the King of glory shall come in. Who is this King of glory? The Lord Yeshua, He is the King of glory" thundered Moses just as loudly.

And as God's Two Witnesses began to testify to Israel of the true identity of their long-awaited Messiah, the armed contingent guarding the Temple Mount surrounded them and ordered them to cease their preaching, threatening to kill them if they didn't.

"The Lord is my light and my salvation; whom shall I fear? The Lord is the strength of my life; of whom shall I be afraid? When the wicked, even my enemies and my foes, came upon me to eat up my flesh, they stumbled and fell" replied Moses.

At this, the guards fired their rifles at the Two Witnesses, emptying full clips. To their utter astonishment, the Two Witnesses still stood there, unaffected by the hail of bullets that seemed to just pass right through them.

Elijah looked heavenward saying "Hear me, O LORD, hear me, that Your people may know that you are the LORD God, and that You are turning their heart back again".

Immediately, in response, a bluish fire fell from Heaven and completely consumed the attacking contingent, their weapons, and even the dust beneath their feet. Nothing was left that could even signify that there were people standing there just a moment ago. No clothing. No blood. Nothing.

The Israeli PM was thoroughly

impressed with the Chancellor. Not only did Prince Faakhir seem to know the entire history of the struggle of the Jewish people, but he was even acutely aware of the actual dates of important events, milestones, and tragedies experienced by them as well. It was this intimate knowledge of his people that caused the PM to put his trust, and the safety of Israel into the hands of the Chancellor. He marveled at the relative ease in which this latest peace initiative - The International Peace Accord, negotiated by Prince Faakhir to last for seven years - established peace not only in the Middle East, but globally. Major hot-spots all over the world appeared to diffuse quickly - seemingly almost overnight. Prince Faakhir also stopped the hemorrhaging of the world financial markets by instituting a one-world currency based on the euro. But most importantly, genocide, attempted genocide, all hate crimes and crimes against humanity were now vigorously prosecuted in the International Criminal Court - which meant no more genocide-bombers sneaking into Israel to blow up defenseless men, women and children. And - having parted the land to gain a lasting peace - as part of the treaty they were now able to rebuild their Temple. The PM was amazed at how quickly the world was changing - all due to the vision and leadership of the Chancellor. He watched the A/V monitors as UNN continued live coverage of the removal of the huge walls built by Israel to keep out genocide-bombers. This, he thought to himself, was truly a New World Order. Suddenly, the network interrupted with a breaking-news report. It was showing the footage taken by a tourist of an incident on the Temple Mount which occurred just minutes ago. The PM's jaw dropped as they repeated the footage over and over again.

"Now what!?" queried the perplexed PM.

Ant, Joey, Miriam, and Sarah were huddled in the midst of Sarah's living room floor poring over the trunk-load of materials that Ant and Sarah brought back with them nearly two weeks ago.

"I don't know 'bout you guys", half-whispered Ant, "but I'm beginnin' to believe that everything these bible prophecy DVDs and books are telling us is true. I mean, who could deny it. It's happenin' right before our eyes! The vanishings, the one-world currency, the 7-year peace treaty, the rebuilding of the Temple, and now a one-world government ruled by a 'world chancellor'!"

"I must admit that it would seem that many prophecies from our Torah - your Old Testament - and from your New Testament, do fit the events transpiring these days. However, I'm still a little hesitant to acknowledge that Yeshua - that's Jesus to you - is the Messiah. My people have always denied that He was the Holy One of Israel, but the evidence to the contrary is quite overwhelming. My God, if it is true, what do we do now? What do we do?"

Suddenly the room was filled with an ethereal glow as Arizael appeared in their midst.

"Don't be afraid, but be encouraged", spoke Arizael to all.

"Sweet Jesus!" exclaimed Ant as he jumped, startled, as was everyone else by Ariel's unexpected insertion into time.

"Yes, He is that and more. My name is Arizael. I am here to help you during the Tribulation Period, although you won't be seeing much of me until the second half - the Great Tribulation".

"Then it is true", said Joey, still shaking a little. "The DVDs, the books, and ...oh my God...Yeshua was...is..."

"Yes, Yeshua is Lord. The Alpha and the Omega. Son of the Most High God. The Lamb of God. The Christ. The Lord God Almighty, and the soon returning Messiah, King of Kings and Lord of Lords. Amen.

"What should we do?" asked Miriam, who held a tight grip on Joey's arm.

"Repent of your sins and acknowledge Yeshua as both Lord and Savior for you are His own", replied Arizael.

Without a moment's hesitation, all four went to their knees, and in humble submission, asked the Lord to forgive their sins and acknowledged Him as Lord of their lives. Immediately they were filled with the Holy Spirit as the room was saturated with His anointing presence.

"You have been empowered for service unto our King and for His Kingdom. Study the

Word of God continuously. Go and listen to God's Two Witnesses, Elijah and Moses, who are stationed on the Temple Mount. Pray with and for one another without ceasing, and always remember that no matter how dark the days ahead may appear - and they will, our God reigns. He is - how you say - 'Large and In Charge'. Shalom." said Arizael, smiling, as he encouraged their souls. He then stepped back into eternity and out of their plane of natural vision.

The four began to give thanks and praise unto God, and as they were ascribing all glory and honor to Him and to His Son Yeshua, the house began to shake from the presence of the Spirit of God.

<u>Chapter 5</u>

"And thou shalt come up
against my people of Israel,
as a cloud to cover the land;
it shall be in the latter days,
and **I** will bring thee against My land,
that the nations may know **Me**,
when **I** shall be sanctified in thee,
O Gog, before their eyes."
- Ezekiel 38:16

Heaven was filled with activity, joy, and anticipation. Everything was executed with flawless perfection. Myriads of angels came and went, as they carried out their assignments according to the will of the Lord. In the Throne Room, all eyes were upon the Lord as He unscrolled the title deed to the Earth a little further until He came to the second seal. Lightnings, thunders, and voices emanated from the midst of the Throne as the Lord opened the second seal.

The Russian Premier leaned back in his leather-upholstered chair, pondering thoughts he naively believed to be his own. Unbeknownst to him, there were demons constantly whispering in his ear, of evil plots and diabolical plans.

"This could work. This could really work, if - and only if, we all work together, and I'm sure Israel's enemies would gladly join with me. If we time it right, no one will be able to stop us" he mused as an evil smirk appeared on his face. He then ordered his aide to set up a secret conference call with the leaders of most of Israel's surviving enemies in the Middle East, especially Iran. Within two hours, the aide had them all on the line.

Gentlemen", he said as he began his call, "As you know, the U.S. has set a great precedent for "invading" a sovereign nation that has been perceived as a great threat to global peace and security, especially a nation possessing WMD. I have a great proposition for you".

Ant, Joey, Sarah, and Miriam had just concluded their daily bible study with prayer and thanksgiving. They now began to discuss the current world situation.

"I think that we have already experienced the opening of the first seal which is the rise of the Antichrist, whom I personally believe is Prince Faakhir Abdul-Waahid" stated Ant matter-of-factly.

"I thought that the Antichrist comes out of the EU. Prince Faakhir is from Syria" said Joey.

"Well, the Scriptures calls the Antichrist 'the Assyrian' and says he is '*of* the PEOPLE that shall come', meaning that at least one person in his lineage is of Roman ancestry. Remember, the Roman Empire included present-day Syria and Jordan. Prince Faakhir has both Assyrian and Roman roots" replied Ant.

"Okay, so what's going to happen next?" asked Miriam, not really sure if she truly wanted to hear the answers if there were any.

It was quiet for a moment as they looked from one to another.

"The opening of the second seal which is, I'm afraid, an all-out attack on Israel that leads to nuclear war", replied Ant.

"Right. Ezekiel - chapters 38 and 39!" said Joey excitedly.

"Oh no! Shouldn't we try to get out of here before it happens?" exclaimed Sarah.

"Not to worry. This is where the Lord begins to once again magnify Himself to Israel and all the nations on the earth. He Himself will defend Israel and sanctify His holy Name", replied Ant assuringly. "The Lord of Hosts will defend Israel".

"Of that I have absolutely no doubt," said Joey, "however, I do believe that we should continue stockpiling as much food as possible, even accelerating it as fast as we can because we know what's coming down the road. I'll also see if I can acquire a supply of iodine pills, just in case".

"Just in case? In case of what?" asked Sarah.

"Radiation poisoning," answered Ant somewhat solemnly, as they headed out to obtain additional supplies.

Although it would seem to the casual observer that chaos was reigning in the Jet Propulsion Laboratory (JPL) at NASA, the truth was totally the opposite. Everyone was on point and giving their utmost attention to whatever it was that they doing at every moment.

Ever since he had received Dr. Wersop's phone call, Dr. Tom McKnight had been one busy and fearfully excited astrophysicist. He had been unable to get in contact with Dr. Wersop since the disappearances, but he didn't let that stop him from his work. He had confirmed Dr. Wersop's findings and relayed them to the Pentagon, who then notified the

White House, and although the President ordered the situation to be classified Top Secret and a matter of National Security so as not to create a public panic, the White House also informed the Chancellor of the World Union.

Early in the morning of the 9th of Av, citizens all over Israel were awakened by the loud sirens of a warning klaxon. Seconds later, Joey's cell phone began to ring. It was the PM's office notifying him that two missiles were inbound - ETA 3 minutes. They had also received reports of what appeared to be a huge sandstorm headed their way across the desert. Joey's orders were to take shelter immediately and to report back if, and when, he could.

Meanwhile, high above the Earth, two Chinese-built Russian SS-27 missiles separated their 2nd stages and fired their 3rd stages as they began to reenter the atmosphere directly above northern and southern Israel respectively.

Seconds after reentry, the two warheads detonated, miles above the Holy Land. For a moment there were two new suns high in the morning sky, great blinding flashes of light, but down below there was no physical damage whatsoever from the twin blasts. That was by design. These missiles weren't sent to destroy property, but rather to negate the possibility of response to what was coming next. No, the purpose of these missiles was to produce an electromagnetic pulse (EMP) effect, which in turn would disable any and every electrical, electronic, and motorized system in the affected area, thereby completely nullifying any type of defensive response that Israel would try to mount. The detonations produced the desired effects perfectly. Moments later, all power was lost throughout Israel. Everything was down, and Israel, for all practical purposes, was defenseless, and to make matters worse, one of the last reports to come in before power was lost stated that the sandstorm was actually the dust raised by 2,500,000 heavily armed men, with many on horseback, and dozens of armored tank divisions racing toward the borders of Israel from the North, the South, and the East.

Meanwhile, simultaneously in the U.S., suicide sleeper cells in twelve bi-coastal cities detonated their black market-purchased Russian-made nuclear suitcase bombs, effectively bringing the country to a complete standstill and causing the U.S., which was still reeling from the hard-hitting effects of the Rapture on its government and overall population, to stagger from the effects of God's judgment on her.

Will, along with the rest of the Bride of Christ, stood before the Throne and listened as the Father spoke to His Son.

"Gog is come up against My people, and now My fury has come up in My face. Therefore O God, Your God shall send a great confusion upon the invading army and every man's sword shall be against his brother. I shall rain an overflowing rain upon them, and great hailstones, fire, and brimstone. Thus will I magnify Myself, and sanctify Myself; and I will be known in the eyes of many nations, and they shall know that I am the LORD".

Everyone in Heaven gave glory, honor, and praise to God saying, "Holy, Holy, Holy, LORD God Almighty".

The Israeli PM could only stand still and watch as the approaching hordes came closer and closer into view. Without any power sources whatsoever, Israel was unable to deploy, contact, or even alert their forces to defend against the invasion. As he watched from the top of Mt. Olivet with a pair of binoculars, he slowly became aware of a noticeable decrease in the amount of sunlight. He took the binoculars from his eyes and looked to the sky. Out of a clear blue sky, he saw enormous black roiling clouds form out over the desert above the invading armies. Even as he watched, darkness began to cover the desert and great peals of thunder crashed and huge bolts of lightning streaked from the heavens to the desert, finding a target every time. The heavens opened and a deluge of heavy rain began to pummel the invading hosts. Immediately, the invaders became disoriented, and as tempers and fears mounted, they began to fight amongst themselves. The Israeli PM could not believe what he was witnessing. He watched as watermelon-sized hailstones began to pulverize the bands of men. The scene appeared otherworldly. The howls and wails that rose up from the desert seemed to emanate from Hell itself. Then, just when the Israeli PM thought "he had seen it all", he watched awestruck, as fire and brimstone rained from the sky upon the remnant of the invading armies. He witnessed as their flesh fell from their skeletons while they were yet standing upon their feet. Their screams chilled him to the bone. Then - deathly silence. As quickly as it had begun, it was over. The skies cleared, and the sunlight returned to reveal the scope and the magnitude of the destruction of their enemies. The PM stood shaking as he surveyed the carnage before him as the remaining one-sixth of the invading hosts retreated and fled in deathly fear. He then lifted his eyes toward the heavens and joined the thousands, who had also witnessed the miraculous deliverance, in worshiping and giving all the praise and glory to the Lord God of Israel. At that moment, all electrical and electronic power was restored to Israel, even to equipment that should never have operated again due to the EMP effect. As communications were now restored, news of the miraculous event spread like wildfire throughout Israel and the world. News also came that at the time Israel was being defended by God, fire and brimstone also fell upon Russia and upon those nations that came up with her against the land of Israel. No one on Earth could deny that the Lord God of Israel had fought for His people, and everyone now knew, if they didn't know before, that Israel still is, and always will be, the apple of God's eye.

However short the conflagration was in Israel, the rest of the world, indeed was not as fortunate. Nations on whom the Lord had showered fire and brimstone, having mistakenly assumed that their enemies had launched missiles against them, now launched their few remaining missiles in supposed retribution. Unfortunately, unbeknownst to them was the fact that their enemies, especially the United States of America, still had their entire arsenal of nukes and the ability to launch them, and in response, many were on their deadly accurate way.

It was the shortest war ever, time-wise. One day. However it was the most destructive and deadliest war ever. Nearly two billion people dead. Millions were injured, many critically, with nuclear fallout and radiation poisoning affecting millions more. However, not a single missile fell within Israel due to her Missile Defense Shield (and the Lord's hand, of course), nor did any radiation enter into the land.

The nations that came against Israel, for all practical purposes, virtually ceased to exist, having suffered double blows, due to both their ignorance and lack of understanding. The rest of the nations began the daunting task of rebuilding that which had been destroyed, if at all possible, and the cremating of their dead.

<u>Chapter 6</u>

> "...for the Lord hath called
> for a famine…" - *2 Kings 8:1*

The Body of Christ watched in awe and wonder at the events transpiring there and on the Earth below. They sat with their gaze transfixed toward the Throne of God as the Lord Yeshua opened the third seal. As he did so, there came a voice out of the midst of the four living creatures saying:

"A measure of wheat for a penny, and three measures of barley for a penny; and see thou hurt not the oil and wine".

Ant, Joey, and the women had just finished their daily bible study and prepared to watch a DVD on the subject of The End Times. It had been two weeks since the surprise attack on Israel. Joey observed his sister Sarah as she saw to Ant's comfort and he quietly brought Miriam's attention to it as well. It wasn't long before Ant and Sarah noticed the big grins on Joey and Miriam's faces.

"What? What are you two grinnin' about?" asked Ant, all the while smiling from ear to ear himself.

"Ohhh nothing, nothing at all", replied Joey with a happy laugh.

"Yeah right. Don't give us that, you two. What's so amusing? We want to know. Now 'fess up!" said Sarah.

Miriam stood and walked over to them and said," We're just so glad that you two have bonded together so nicely, and, well, we're very happy for the two of you!"

Ant and Sarah stared at each other for a second before looking back at the other two.

"Is it really that obvious?" asked Sarah, somewhat sheepishly.

"Are you kidding? A blind person could see it!" laughed Joey.

"Ha-ha. Very funny, *bro*, and I mean that in every sense of the word", replied Ant, grinning just as hard.

"What do you mean? "What are you saying?" asked Joey as he looked from Ant to Sarah and back to Ant again.

Ant and Sarah clasped hands as Sarah said to Ant, "Go on. Tell them. Now is as good a time as any".

Ant announced, "Sarah and I have decided to get married!"

Joey stood stunned for a second, and then rushed and hugged his sister with great joy. He then hugged Ant and shook his hand with great exuberance. Miriam gave Ant a congratulatory kiss and then enveloped Sarah with a seemingly never-ending embrace.

"Wow, this is so amazing", said Joey, as he and Miriam stood together and embraced. "I say that because we also have decided to tie the knot".

At that, the hugs and kisses began anew, and the room was filled with an air of love, joy and affection.

"This calls for a celebration. Let's go out

to dinner!" exclaimed Joey. "I know a nice little restaurant. Sorta romantic, and the food's not bad either!"

"Sounds like a winner to me. It'll be good just to get out of the house for a short while. You know, our God is so great; it's a blessing just to be able to go outdoors without having to worry about things like radiation poisoning. The Lord truly keeps Israel. Bless His Holy Name", said Ant.

Each of the others responded with an "Amen" as they headed to the door - all of them filled with excitement and joy. Unseen by them, their guardian angels followed them, hovering close to each of their charges, with swords at the ready.

The group arrived at the restaurant without incident, and sat down to enjoy a sumptuous meal. On one of the many monitors situated throughout the restaurant was the telecast from UNN. They were reporting on the status of the ever-increasing worldwide famine crisis and the apparent inability of the nations to stem its tide. Millions were starving and hundreds of thousands were dying as a result of the famine, which of course itself was the result of the destruction from the War of

Gog and Magog.

"Almost makes you feel guilty about being able to come here and enjoy a good meal" said Ant, to no one in particular.

"Yeah, I know what you mean", replied Joey.

"Hey guys, I understand what you're saying, but we're here to celebrate, so let's celebrate!" interjected Miriam.

"Absolutely. Let us give thanks to the Lord for not only saving us, but also for preserving us and providing for us! God has blessed Israel yet again and will continue to do great and mighty things. Oh, forever bless the name of Yeshua!" exclaimed Sarah, with glass upraised.

"Amen. Amen." responded the others as they also lifted their glasses and gave thanks unto the Lord their God.

The Israeli PM listened intently as the

World Chancellor finished his speech at the UN (which was now located in Babylon, Iraq due to the nuking of New York City). The Chancellor was calling on all the nations of the world to put aside their "petty differences for the sake of the survival of mankind". He was referring to, (and all the while making a case for enforcing), the world peace treaty in which
every nation on earth had signed a non-aggression pact and swore to solemnly uphold and enforce it against all violators. What had so caught the PM's attention was the repeated stipulations that the peace treaty, which was officially to span one heptad (seven years), would guarantee Israel complete security and sanction to rebuild their Temple.

"and so, in closing, ladies and gentlemen...no..., sisters and brothers - for we are one family in the earth. Mother Earth is our only home and we must protect her and ourselves from further harm and danger. Together we can forge a New Age for mankind, free of war and poverty, where all mankind can live in peace and prosperity. Will you follow me? Will you let me lead you to our utopia? One Earth. One Family. One World. Together, we can do anything! Thank You!"

said the Chancellor as he finished his moving speech. It was strangely very reminiscent of the highly charismatic speeches that Adolf Hitler used to give to Nazi Germany. Nevertheless, it was met with a long thunderous applause from everyone present, which lasted at least ten minutes.

The Israeli PM still, even now, could hardly believe what he was hearing, even though he had heard it before. Finally. Peace for Israel and a rebuilt Temple where they could worship the Lord their God who had just recently shown Himself mighty to save.

"This must be the Lord's work", said the PM to himself. "Who else could bring these things to pass? I must call a meeting immediately". He began to walk as quickly as possible through the thronging crowd towards his office at the U.N.

Suddenly, in a vision, he was transported to the Temple Mount in Jerusalem where he stood before the Lord's Two Witnesses. As he came near, the Two Witnesses addressed the Israeli PM.

"You have made a covenant with death, and with hell are you at agreement" proclaimed Moses.

"Your covenant with death shall be disannulled, and your agreement with hell shall not stand" thundered Elijah.

"W-What do you mean by that?" asked the PM.

Just as suddenly, the Israeli PM was back in Babylon, justifiably dazed by what had just transpired. He slowly resumed his trek to his U.N. office, wondering what to make of his experience.

Ant and Joey were loading more supplies into the basement when Joey's cellphone chirped. Joey glanced at the text message and said to Ant, "The PM's called an important meeting. Let's go. While I grab my stuff, will you let the girls know what's up and where we're going?"

"Sure, no problem. Be back in a minute", replied Ant as he raced upstairs to inform Sarah and Miriam of the situation. True to his word, he was back in a minute and he joined Joey in the car as they sped off to the Knesset.

"Did they say what the meeting was about?" asked Ant.

"No. The only thing that they would say was that it was very important...so important that the PM flew back in order to have this meeting as soon as possible. I know that Prince Faakhir addressed the UN this morning, but I haven't yet listened to the news or anything today. I wonder what's going on", replied Joey.

"Well, it appears that we are about to find out", said Ant as the car quickly approached their destination. They hustled from the car to the gate where they were immediately given entrance. They were quickly escorted to the Knesset's main assembly chamber, where they were speedily seated, as the meeting was about to commence. The PM, seated across the room within a group of serious-minded men, stood to speak.

"Gentlemen. I have convened this meeting to consider a matter of utmost importance and urgency. I have just returned from the U.N., where I had the privilege to hear the Chancellor speak and reiterate his stalwart support for the World Peace Initiative and for Israel, as well. The Chancellor is intimately aware of the struggle and suffering of our people and of the need for us to feel secure in our own land. I have discussed the current situation with, among others, members of the Temple Institute, and with great joy I can inform all of you here present, that next month the rebuilding of Solomon's Temple will safely resume with 'round-the-clock construction shifts due to the peace provided by Prince Faakhir."

The air became electric at that announcement. Conversations flew from one side of the Knesset to the other. Ant and Joey exchanged knowing glances with each other.

"Gentlemen... Gentlemen, please", said the PM as he quieted the excited assembly. "We begin this momentous work with the approval, not only of our esteemed World Chancellor, but of the entire World Union. The Temple itself shall be a symbol of the new Peace Accord. We shall finally again have our Temple in the midst of our people."

The room exploded with queries for the PM, most of which he answered as fully as he could. Ant and Joey sat through the entire proceeding, deciding to glean as much information as was available. An hour later, they departed and headed back to the house.

Joshua Cohen (or J.C. as he preferred to be called) was nearly at his wit's end. He had endured all that he could take. He knew that his parents were killed when New York City was nuked and he had just now watched his sister die of radiation poisoning and malnutrition. He was angry. He was angry at the world, and at God. Especially God. How could He have let this happen, he wondered to himself. He stumbled through the Emergency Trauma Center and onto the streets of Abington, Pa., leaving the hospital where his sister had just passed away. He was becoming more disoriented by the minute; his grief combining with his anger and hunger made him dizzy. He sat down on the curb and lay back onto the grass. As he lay there peering into an empty sky, a thought came to him. As he contemplated the thought, the first flicker of hope appeared in his eyes.

"Yes. Yes, I will. I will return to Israel. I will return home. There's no reason to remain on vacation here in the U.S. There's nothing left here for me but anguish of the soul. I will return to my homeland", he half-whispered with teary eyes.

His mind began to clear as he made his way back to Valet Parking to get his car. Two minutes seemed like an eternity as he waited while the valet retrieved his vehicle and pulled up before him. He got in the car, slowly pulled out and headed south on Old York Rd. (Rte. 611) towards his sister's condo in Mt. Airy, with tears streaming down his face.

Chapter 7

"And I looked, and behold a pale horse:
and his name that sat on him was Death,
and Hell followed with him."
- Revelation 6:8

Will and Ruby, along with all the other
Saints, watched in complete and utter awe as
the Lord Yeshua Christ opened the fourth seal.
The almost overwhelming beauty and serenity
of Heaven stood in stark contrast to the events
now occurring on the Earth. As a result of the
short but catastrophic nuclear exchanges, a
large portion of the world's population had
been wiped out. Although most died directly
from the war, many millions died as a result of
the war's effect - namely radiation poisoning,
famine, and pestilence. The inhabitants of
Heaven watched as Hell enlarged itself as over
a billion souls steadily poured into it.

Will recognized one of the damned falling
into the inferno. It was Reverend Durite. Will

recalled him from a dead church that he had visited a couple of times. He remembered how it rubbed him the wrong way that Rev. Durite preached that *good works* were a requirement to not only obtain salvation, but to keep it as well - *not* trusting in the finished work of Christ at Calvary. The Word of God came to Will's mind as he witnessed Rev. Durite's descent into everlasting darkness. "There is a way *(religion)* that seemeth right unto a man, but the end thereof *are* the ways of death" - Proverbs 14:12.

Rev. Durite screamed in terror as the tunnel of light he'd been traveling through suddenly turned into a tunnel of flames, through which he was rapidly falling. His terror increased even more as he could now see the pit of Hell far below as he speedily rushed towards it. His mind raced as madness slowly gripped him.

"*How* could this *be*? I'm a Christian!" his

tortured mind kept pondering. "I'm a *good* person! I've *kept* the Ten Commandments! Why am *I* here? God, You've made a *mistake*!"

Rev. Durite's descent came to an abrupt halt as he joined billions of others in the bowels of Hell. He could *see* nothing, as there was no light of any kind whatsoever - even the flames were pitch black and gave no light. He could *hear* however, and the cacophony of the damned rose up to unbearable levels. He could hear the screams, and the wailing, and the gnashing of teeth together due to pain. He could also *smell*. The odor of sulfur (brimstone) sickened him and made him want to vomit, but he couldn't. And he could *feel*. He felt the flames. He felt the worms. But even worse than these - he felt the complete absence of the presence of God - and all hope was lost - forever. As his mind grasped the truth of this thought, Rev. Durite lost his sanity and began to wail for all eternity.

———————————————

J. C. marveled at the miracle before his

eyes. He surveyed the blossoming desert - nearly in full bloom - from his high-rise apartment in Jerusalem. He had been back home for nearly a month now, and he could still hardly believe this view. Although he was happy to be back in the land of his fathers, he was sad that his family wasn't here with him. His eyes looked heavenward, beyond the blue skies, searching...pondering...wondering why God had allowed all this misery and sorrow to befall him. He was no longer angry with God; he just wanted to know "why?" He supposed that he would never know the answer to that question, so he decided not to dwell on it. Instead, he began to think about his new job as an office assistant at the Knesset. He was excited about his new position and he was prepared to pour his entire being into it - in an attempt to try to fill the huge gaping hole in his heart.

Ant, Sarah, Joey and Miriam had decided

on a double wedding. They were currently in the process of making plans for same when UNN began airing the world news. The report was basically the same every night - stories of people all over the world dying by the millions due to starvation and radiation poisoning. Every country was affected in some way or another - every one, that is, except for one - Israel. Israel was the only nation on Earth where the air was completely clean and clear. It was also the only place where there was an abundance of food, and all the other nations were keenly aware of it. Israel, by virtue of this fact, was quickly becoming the most prosperous - and most hated - nation in the world.

"My God! It looks like the fourth seal has been opened!" exclaimed Ant, as all turned their attention to the monitor. The grisly and ghastly scenes of death and despair that filled the screen were almost more than they could bear to watch. There was report after report from different nations of hundreds of mass graves being filled with thousands of bodies. There was just so much death. In fact, it was being widely reported by UNN, going by conservative estimates alone, that at least one-fourth of the world's population had been decimated as the result of the war, worldwide famine, and pandemic diseases.

"Lord, we thank you for Your great grace and mercy toward us", prayed Joey in a half-whisper.

"Amen" confessed the others in unison as they began to give thanks and praise unto the Lord for His providence, protection, and provision. They were especially thankful that they had met a small group of fellow believers some weeks ago. They were glad for the fellowship because the world's hatred of both the Jews and believers in Christ seemed to be increasing exponentially every day. The believers were constantly being accused of "hate crimes" simply because they would not approve of, nor live by, the current society's amoral values and laws. For example, it was now a "hate crime" if you tried to "proselytize" someone who didn't share your worldview. In other words, if you were caught witnessing to someone about the great work of redemption that was wrought by Yeshua, the Christ, to reconcile man back to God, you would be arrested, charged, and prosecuted for committing a "hate crime", never mind the fact that what you were doing was out of genuine love and caring for the individual. This mind-set of society was not new at all however, because even before the Rapture occurred, these attitudes, laws, and court rulings began to rear their ugly heads. Only now, no longer restrained by the Holy Spirit, they were coming into full fruition.

"I feel that we should keep the ceremony small", said Ant, getting back to the business at hand.

"I agree", replied Joey, "...just us and "The Congregation"(which was how the body of believers had begun to refer to themselves). We don't want to draw too much attention to ourselves."

They all nodded in agreement and then began rejoicing about the upcoming nuptials. They put out of their minds (for the moment) any and all fears concerning the persecution of believers, which was growing ever more pernicious with each passing day. They had even begun to hear stories of mass executions taking place in some parts of the European Union, Middle East, and Far East. Of course, the New World Order-controlled media wasn't even reporting these atrocities, much less confirming them. Even still, there seemed to be many eyewitness accounts of hundreds, perhaps thousands of believers who had been beheaded because of their refusal to renounce their faith in the Lord Yeshua and join the **W**orld **E**cumenical **Re**ligion (WE'RE), which denies that Yehovah is God (I Am), but rather teaches that *all* are gods (WE ARE).

The glorious Body of Christ sat before the Father's throne, ascribing the greatest praise, glory and honor unto Him. Christ the Lord had just moments ago opened the fifth seal, and no sooner had He done so, there began to appear under the altar in Heaven, the souls of those Tribulation period believers who were beheaded for their testimony of Yeshua. Thousands of souls dressed in white robes, appearing continuously, began to cry out in a loud voice, "How long, O Lord, holy and true, dost thou not judge and avenge our blood on them that dwell on the earth?" The Father, in an authoritative, yet lovingly calming voice said to them, "Rest yet for a little season, until the number of your fellow servants also and your brethren, that should be killed as you were, is fulfilled."

The Body of Christ, in wondrous awe of the love and patience of the Father, watched as thousands more souls steadily arrived in Heaven.

Erik Johnson trembled slightly as he was led towards the front of the line at the Community Compliance Center (CCC). He thought of his wife and children who were in hiding and more than likely fearing what had become of him. It was just yesterday that he had ventured out to try and locate some food for his family. He had managed to get in touch with his cousin, who told him to come by and get some help. When he arrived, however, all he found waiting for him was the police, whom his cousin had alerted of his pending arrival. That was yesterday, and now…now he was sure that he had seen his family for the last time this side of Heaven. He prayed silently that the Lord would continue to give him strength to stand to the end. They had tortured and questioned him all night long, but he gave them no information. His family was still safe in God's hands and it was them, not himself, he was praying for as he finally reached the front of the line.

"#&%@% vermin, this is your last chance. Will you renounce Yeshua as Lord, and join the rest of society in our great World Union? You and your kind are the last holdouts. Why do you all resist? Haven't you heard - 'Resistance is futile'. You can't win. Renounce Yeshua now! If you do, we promise not to kill you and your family. Oh yes, we captured them last night, as well. You do want to save them, don't you?" sneered the Officer in Charge (OIC).

Erik knew in his spirit that they were lying about his family, but that didn't matter anyway because the Lord spoke to his spirit and said, "Fear not them that kill the body, but are not able to kill the soul: but rather fear Him which is able to destroy both body and soul in Hell".

Erik replied, looking the officer right dead in his eyes, "They are already saved, and know this, 'that at the name of Yeshua, every knee in Heaven, on Earth, and under the earth shall bow; and every tongue shall confess that Yeshua, the Christ, is Lord, to the glory of God the Father'. Amen."

At this, the demons within the OIC became enraged. The officer violently punched Erik in the abdomen, causing him to double over in pain. The officer then maliciously brought his club down with full force to connect with the back of Erik's head. Blood splattered onto the officer and his club, as Erik collapsed to the floor. He was still alive, although his breathing came in labored gasps for air.

"Take him. He's yours", said the OIC as he motioned to the executioners to come and take him away.

Erik was nearly unconscious as they took him, but he was very aware of the excruciating pain that seemed to wreak havoc through every nerve in his body. His spirit though, was in perfect peace.

"Just a few more moments...and all will be well. I'm coming home, Lord Yeshua", he quietly prayed, looking up toward the heavens.

As the executioner's sword began to fall, Erik heard the Lord's reply in his spirit, "My son, come on home", and he smiled.

All the Israeli PM could do was shake his head in awesome wonder. The sight of the nearly completed Temple, although still a work in progress, was nevertheless extraordinarily breathtaking. It was quickly becoming by all standards the most magnificent edifice in the world, and it was theirs. The PM watched as the Temple priests went about their daily oblations, which they had re-instituted just a few months ago. It amazed him that they were finally at peace with their neighboring nations and again offering sacrifices in their Temple. How proud he was that the World Chancellor himself was coming in a couple of months to visit the Temple, which was only appropriate, since it was Prince Faakhir's peace treaty that made the safe and quick rebuilding of the Temple possible in the first place.

"Lord God of Israel, God of our fathers Abraham, Isaac, and Jacob, we give you praise and glory!" exulted the PM as he reluctantly abandoned the wondrous view from his office window.

Chapter 8

> "And the kings of the earth...
> said to the mountains and rocks,
> Fall on us, and hide us from the face
> of Him that sits on the throne,
> and from the wrath of the Lamb:
> For the great day of His wrath is come;
> and who shall be able to stand?"
> *- Revelation 6:15-17*

It was becoming increasingly more dangerous by the day for Joey and Ant at the Knesset. Joey had hired Ant as his "Personal Assistant" and as the weeks grew into months, they and their fellow believers watched as Israel and the rest of the world fell for the deceptions of the Antichrist - hook, line and sinker. Most of the employees could "feel" that Joey and Ant weren't 100% behind the "program", and a few of them even began to wonder what it was about these two that made them so "different". One of these was J.C., and he made it a point to find out. A very direct point. One day, after work, he followed them as they headed towards home. Ant, realizing that they were being followed, alerted Joey to the same and began driving away from the direction of the house. J.C., recognizing that he had "been made", then began to blow the car horn and motioning for Ant to pull over and stop.

"I don't know who this guy is, but he looks vaguely familiar", said Ant, looking into the rear view mirror, as he slowly began to pull the car over.

J.C. carefully pulled in behind them so as not to cause them any further alarm. He got out of his car slowly and put a smile on his face.

"Hey guys, I'm not trying to do anything. I just want to ask you two a few questions, that's all. I hope you don't mind".

"Depends", replied Ant, being somewhat suspicious.

" *'Depends'*. Depends on what?" asked J.C.

"Depends on the motives of a guy who tried to covertly follow us", answered Joey, as he eyed J.C. and tried to remember where he'd seen him before.

"My name is Joshua. Joshua Cohen, but

my friends…"- he hesitated, remembering that most of his friends were now dead, killed in the nuclear strikes against the U.S. - "everyone calls me J.C. I also work at the Knesset as do you".

"Okay, that's where I've seen you before. So, how can we help you and why were you following us like that?" inquired Joey.

"I…I just wanted to ask you guys something", began J.C. "I've noticed that you guys seem to have, for whatever reasons I don't know, some reservations about the direction in which the government is taking our country. I also sense something else, but I just can't put my finger on it. There is something different about the two of you from anyone else I've ever met, personally or professionally, and that is why I followed you. I want to know what that 'something' is."

Ant and Joey just looked at each other and smiled.

"Okay, we'll tell you - after we've had dinner. Follow us. I'm sure you know how to do that", said Joey with a smile.

"Thanks", replied J.C., somewhat embarrassedly, as he headed for his car.

A few minutes later, all were back on the road, as Ant and Joey headed for home with

J.C. bringing up the rear.

———————————————

It was dark as midnight in the Russian Premier's hidden underground conference chamber. It was darker still in his heart. He was still stewing in anger even though it had been nearly three and a half years since they had been thoroughly humiliated by the Hebrew God in the Israeli desert. As he sat in darkness, thinking upon the total destruction of five-sixths of the Russian/Islamic forces, and the resultant deliverance of Israel, like Pharaoh of old, his heart hardened even more.

"I will not rest until they are destroyed. Not until every single Jew is wiped off the face of the earth", he seethed between clenched teeth. "And anyone who tries to get in my way will suffer also" said he as he unknowingly repeated what the two demons at his sides planted into his heart.

He then buzzed his aide and told him to page the commanders of the armed forces that were remaining and have them report immediately to his chamber. He sat motionless, staring into the blackness of the room, until the last of the summoned commanders had arrived outside his chamber.

"Lights, 66 percent", he spoke into the darkness. Gradually, the room was illuminated to two-thirds of its maximum brightness. He then signaled his aide to send in the commanders. After they filed into the room and stood at attention, he put them at ease and said, "Comrades, Mother Russia has need of us!"

J. C. stood at a crossroads. Well, actually he was *sitting* on the edge of the recliner's seat in the den. The evening had been amazing. Dinner had been outstanding, and the conversation that followed was mesmerizing to say the least. Prophecies. Rapture of the Church. Battle of Gog and Magog. Four

Horsemen of the Apocalypse. Personal angelic visitation?! And everything was to be found right there in the Scriptures, if one took the time to search. Well, he had just been given the scenic tour, and the look on his face was similar to that of a deer caught in the headlights of an oncoming car.

"Okay, I think I follow on all the prophecies, feast days, and their latter-day fulfillments, but what is this 'born-again' business I keep hearing you all mention" J.C. questioned as he sat upright.

Ant grabbed a piece of paper and a Sharpie as he began to answer him. "God created Adam" said Ant as he drew the figure of a humanoid in the top left half of the paper. "Adam sinned, separating himself from God, and incurring the penalty of sin – death and eternity in hell". Ant then drew a line from the figure on the paper horizontally across the top half of the paper. "Now, everyone who was ever born came from Adam who was the Head of the 'old creation' and inherited his sin nature as well as the penalty". Ant then drew another figure on the bottom left half of the paper. "But God loved His own so much that He came down, took on human flesh, lived the sinless, righteous life required by the Law, took our sins upon Himself, paid the penalty for us on the cross, died, was buried, and arose on the third day to be the Head of the 'new creation'". Ant then drew a line from the second figure horizontally across the bottom half of the paper. "As the first Adam was the head of the 'old creation' into which everyone is *physically* born, the "last Adam"- Yeshua, is the Head of the new creation and eternal life and you must be born *spiritually* into it. That is why Yeshua said we must be *'born again'*."

"Ok, now I get it! W-What do I do? I want to be in Yeshua's new creation", said J.C. in a half-whisper.

"What you must do then is repent and ask God to forgive you of your sins, and receive His Son Yeshua as your personal Lord and Savior", replied Joey.

"We'll pray with you if you like", added Ant, to which J.C. nodded his head.

"I'm not very good at praying", confessed J.C. a little sheepishly.

"Neither are we really. In fact, the Bible states that we don't know how to pray as we should, but that the Holy Spirit helps us and prays for us", offered Ant.

"Ok, what do I say?" asked J.C.

"It's really not so important as to what you say, but rather that whatever you say comes from the heart. If you like, I'll lead you in what is called the "sinner's prayer". You repeat after me, and mean it from the heart because you'll be talking to God, not to us. Got it?" said Joey.

"Got it" answered J.C.

"Good. Now, from your heart, in your own words, pray this prayer: 'Lord God Yehovah, Creator of Heaven and Earth, I confess that I am a sinner and I cast myself upon Your mercy. I humbly ask You to forgive me of my sins. I believe that You sent Your Son Yeshua to die for my sins. I believe that He bore my penalty on the cross in my place, died, was buried, and arose the third day, according to the Scriptures. I'm sorry that I've lived my life as if it were my own, to do with it as I pleased. Lord Yeshua, I surrender my life and my will to You, my Lord, my Savior, my Master, and my King. Thank you for Your sacrifice, and Lord, thank you for Your amazing grace, mercy, and unconditional love that You've shown toward me. Thank You so much Lord. Amen, amen, and amen." said Joey.

J.C. repeated the prayer practically verbatim, especially at the beginning, but as he neared the end of the prayer, with tears streaming down his face and a well of peace flooding his soul, he also began to pour out his heart to the Lord. A fire birthed in his heart and spread throughout his spirit. The God-shaped void in his soul was filled perfectly as only God can do. The others joined him as they all began to praise the Lord and give all the glory to God.

Time seemed to whiz by for the members of The Congregation; however, they redeemed every moment of it that they could, knowing what was coming very shortly down the road. They had pooled all their resources and obtained a sizable complex in a very secluded area. This complex had several storage facilities, which they had filled to capacity with non-perishable foods, clothing, light bulbs, flashlights, batteries, gas-powered electric generators, mega-liters of gasoline, and every item they could think of that they would need during the "Great Tribulation" (the last three and a half years of the Tribulation period). The first three and a half years were quickly drawing to a close. Ant and Joey, with their wives, Sarah and Miriam, respectively, had taught The Congregation much about what was soon to befall them, and now the group felt that they were as ready as they would ever be to face the awful times ahead. They knew that secrecy was a great ally, therefore no one discussed the existence or the location of the complex to anyone outside The Congregation, nor were any devices or vehicles with GPS capability allowed within ten miles of the complex. Nature provided a great "shield" with the enormous amount of tall trees, bushes, and shrubbery, and the turn off from the main road onto the "road" that led to the complex, didn't look like a road at all. It was an unmarked gravel trail that appeared to be more of a dead end into the woods, and if you didn't "know" that that was the only possible entrance to the long winding trail that eventually led to the complex, you would drive past it a million times and still not turn there. The complex was very secluded, and with them being on the Lord's side, they felt very secure.

Heaven was …well, Heaven. There was no other way to describe it. Words would fail to even remotely try to express the experience of their new existence. There just wasn't *anything* or *anywhere* that could be compared to it, nor could their new reality be expressed in *any* type of human communication. For the Body of Christ, it was the ultimate "Ya hadda be dere", and they had been here now for nearly three and a half years (Earth-time). Adoration, worship, love, joy, peace, and totally complete fulfillment flowed like a mighty river throughout their entire beings. All of Heaven resonated in perfect harmony as every heavenly being gave glory and honor to God their Creator and to the Lamb in the midst of the throne. All eyes were upon Him as He prepared to open the sixth seal. Every single member of the Redeemed, already nearly overwhelmed with rapturous joy, gazed upon the eternal wounds in the Savior's wrists, as He unrolled the scroll to the next seal. Brilliant light and great glory emanated from all His wounds, and every time they were visible, the Body of Christ was filled with unfathomable gratitude to the Lord. As one, the entire Body of Christ again began to sing "Thou art worthy to take the book, and to open the seals thereof…" As His Body began to worship Him, the Lord Yeshua opened the sixth seal.

The Congregation had just finished having Sunday morning service and most of the members were now engaging in small talk amongst themselves as they stood outside in the pleasant sunshine. Ant, Joey, their wives and a few other members were discussing the timing of the return of the Lord, when Ant thought he saw something out of the corner of his eye. He turned his head slightly so as not to be noticed doing so. Sure enough, he saw an unfamiliar male individual covertly snapping pictures of the Congregation and their premises. Ant soundlessly alerted Joey to the situation with his eyes. Joey acknowledged that he comprehended Ant's alert with a slight nod, and the two of them quietly excused themselves from the conversation and walked ever so casually in the general direction of the young man with the busy camera. As they neared the young man, seemingly about to pass by, Ant yelled "Now' and both he and Joey rushed him, pinning him against a tree.

"Hey— the young man began to protest.

"Hey what" interrupted Ant, snatching the camera out of the young man's hand.

"Who are you and why are you sneaking around taking pictures of us?" asked Joey.

"Let go of me. I don't have to tell you anything.
I said let me go", yelled the young man.

"Not 'til we get some answers", replied Ant, strengthening his hold as the young man tried to break free.

"Again, who are you? What's your name?"

asked Joey, rather forcefully.

Just then a young lady named Elizabeth hurriedly approached them.

"Naman! Naman, what is going on?" queried Beth (as she was called).

"Do you know this person?" Joey asked Beth as she neared them.

"Yes. Yes I do. He's a co-worker of mine from work. What's going on?"

"That's exactly what we would like to know. We caught him covertly taking pictures of our people and our premises" said Ant.

Beth turned and faced the young man, still firmly in the grips of Ant and Joey.

"Naman, what is the meaning of this?" she asked.

"I brought you out here because you said that you were looking for someplace where you could worship Yeshua freely. What's going on?"

Naman laughed. "So sweet and so gullible. I'll tell you what's going on – I'm about to get paid -that's what's going on. The authorities are offering rewards for info on persons or groups of your ilk, and boy – have I hit the motherlode".

"Naman, you can't" exclaimed Beth in

disbelief.

"Oh, but I can, and I will…unless…".

"Unless what?" asked Ant with restrained anger.

"Unless we pay him" answered Joey, also restraining his anger.

"Exact-a-mundo" confirmed Naman, as he began grinning ear-to-ear.

"You pig! I trusted you" cried Beth as her eyes began to well up with tears.

"Like I said – so sweet and so very gullible" replied Naman.

"Let him go" said Ant to Joey as he was about to release his grip on him.

"No, wait" said Beth as she quickly approached them.

In one swift motion, Beth, who had been a star player on her high-school varsity soccer team, delivered a powerful kick to Naman's groin area, eliciting a great howl of pain from him as he crumpled to the ground, no longer being held by Ant and Joey.

"Beth! That's not how Christ would have us react to people or situations like this" scolded Joey.

"True, but He's still working on me. I still have a few rough edges to smooth over I suppose" she replied as she walked away drying her tears.

"Works for me" said Ant with a smile as he removed the flash memory from the camera and dropped the camera by the whimpering Naman.

"Let's go and pray. We'll need the Lord's guidance and ask for His intervention in this matter" suggested Joey.

"Alright, let's go" replied Ant as they both turned and headed to the sanctuary.

Naman continued to whimper as he lay in a tight fetal position for several more minutes. After slightly regaining his composure, Naman began to get up from the ground – slowly. He then stumbled his way to his car, resting against it for a moment before getting in. He immediately started the ignition and floored it, hoping he could recall the way out of the complex.

Beth, looking on from afar, hung her head and wept silently.

The knowledge of the existence of Wersop-1 and Wersop-2, as the fast approaching NEOs had come to be named, had been kept classified as Top Secret information, privy only to the NASA/Pentagon think tank that was working on a nearly completed viable solution and the White House. As it was that both were located in Washington, D.C. when the city was destroyed by a nuclear suitcase bomb, for all intents and purposes, there was now virtually no one aware of the impending cosmic catastrophes. Wersop-1 and Wersop-2 quietly streaked through the vacuum of space towards their divinely-appointed encounters with the Earth.

Naman sped along the highway towards the Allenby Bridge. Still feeling an acute pain in his groin area, he sought to "medicate" himself by smoking a blunt.

"When I get through with them, they'll wish they hadn't laid a finger on me" he said aloud to himself as he reached for his matches, being careful as he neared a bend in the road. Just as he struck and lit the match, Arizael, hovering just above the car, tapped Naman's hand lightly with the very tip of his sword. Naman, not seeing anything, jerked his hand due to the sudden flash of pain, and dropped the match into the seat of the car where he sat. Naman panicked and attempted to locate the match, taking his eyes off the road for five seconds. It proved to be a few seconds too long. In his panicked state, Naman had gradually lost control of his car and crossed the median line in the road, and by the time he realized it, it was already too late. When he looked up and saw the oncoming 18-wheeler, all he had time to say was "Oh, God" before he slipped into eternity to meet Him.

Prince Faakhir, like King Saul of ancient Israel, stood head and shoulders above everyone around him as he walked the tarmac from his official jet – Chancellor 1 – to the terminal. The Israeli PM walked alongside him, having met and welcomed him at the plane. They were engaged in small talk and smiling for all the paparazzi and news reporters. Once inside the terminal and behind closed doors, the conversation turned a little more serious.

Prince Faakhir addressed the PM in almost a scolding manner. "What is this business concerning those so-called "prophets" that preach daily near your Temple? Why haven't you put a stop to their rantings? They've done nothing but brought misery to the whole world…causing droughts by withholding rain and turning water supplies into blood. I don't need any more problems. It takes enough of my time and energy to solve the ones we already have".

"We've tried everything that we know, yet nothing is effective and now the people are beginning to listen and believe what they're saying" replied the PM.

"I guess I'll have to take care of them myself" said Faakhir as they emerged from the room walking towards a waiting limo.

Just then there was a loud scuffle and a scream as an armed man broke through the crowd, pointing a gun at the Chancellor, yelling, "Antichrist!". He was quickly tackled to the ground, but not before he was able to get off one shot. For a moment, the Israeli PM thought that the blood on his jacket was his own, but then as he looked to his left, he realized it was not. Prince Faakhir lay dead of a gunshot wound to his head.

Ant and Joey were both a bit anxious as they addressed the Congregation during the final part of the meeting.

"…since we are only a few days away from the midpoint of the Tribulation Period, and seeing as we know, according to the Scriptures, what's about to happen, it has now come time to leave our compound and head to Petra. We only have three days to move our people.

We've already transported all our compound's supplies earlier this week" informed Joey.

"We'll all move out tomorrow beginning at dawn, so get a good night's rest" instructed Ant.

The Congregation sang a hymn, had prayer and the benediction, and then headed to their homes to get some rest before the big move in the morning.

Ant and Joey sat on the lawn as they both stared up at the starry heavens.

"Enjoy it while you can!" said Ant.

"Huh. What are you talking about" asked Joey

"The grass. The starry sky. Pretty soon, you won't be able to see either from anywhere on Earth" reminded Ant.

"Oh,yeah…that's right. Not until the Kingdom comes. Wow" said Joey.

"Yeah…wow" agreed Ant as they perused the heavens and praised God for His handiwork.

The world had seen nothing like it…ever. The mourning periods of President John F. Kennedy, the Rev. Dr. Martin Luther King Jr., or even Princess Diana paled in comparison to the worldwide outpouring of emotion and grief exhibited during the last couple of days as Prince Faakhir's body lay in state.

On the third day, Faakhir's second-in command, Mark Reubens, a former Israeli prime minister, whom many believers rightly perceived to be the False Prophet, now approached the podium and addressed the millions watching around the world.

"Brothers and sisters of the World Union, I come not with a heavy heart today, but with a joyous one. For you see, this is not the day of an ending, but the dawn of a new day, a new age. It was only a few weeks ago that Prince Faakhir privately revealed his true nature and identity with me, even sharing what would happen to him and what would transpire this day. All of you are blessed to be witnesses of this day. Allow your grief to be turned to joy as you witness the resurrection of your lord and king, the Messiah Faakhir Abdul-Waahid!"

At this pronouncement, Satan entered the

body of the fallen prince and re-animated it. As he did so, there appeared a momentary glow around the body, visible to the human eye. The Antichrist opened his eyes and sat up, much to the utter astonishment and shock of millions worldwide. He then descended from his bier and walked to the podium, hugging the False Prophet, saying to him, "Well done, good and faithful servant". He then turned to the microphone at the podium and declared to the world "I am he that lived, and was dead; and, behold, I live again".

At this proclamation, the audience of viewers worldwide burst into thunderous applause and unrestrained rejoicing as they marveled over their risen lord and king, and began to worship him.

The Congregation began to settle in nicely in Petra. There were several other groups of believers who also had begun making Petra their new home as well. Ant, Joey, and the other leaders of the Congregation met with the leaders of the other groups. All leaders present, there was a total of twelve men – both Jews and Gentiles as to the flesh, but as to the Spirit all were in Christ. They agreed that everyone was equal as servants unto the Lord, but for order's sake that there should be a leader of leaders – an under-shepherd to the Great Shepherd – to the overseeing and wellbeing of the present and soon-to-be-arriving flock of God's people. So they cast lots to choose a leader and the lot fell to one named Yohanan Bar Judah. Yohanan (or John as he was called) accepted the responsibility humbly, giving thanks and praise to God, and asking for His wisdom and blessing to be able to serve faithfully. Then they all laid hands on him and prayed for him as instructed by the Spirit of the Lord, and as they did so, he was imbued with power from on high to serve Him at such a time as this.

Then John spoke to the rest of the leaders saying "Brothers, we know what will transpire here shortly. Let us now prepare to receive God's people who will be fleeing Judea and coming here to Petra. We will come together as a general assembly and break bread together, and then work together to prepare this place as best we can for our arriving brethren".

At this, the leaders returned to their groups and informed them of the developments and everyone made preparation according to the instruction that was given. Thus several groups became one and called themselves the POOR (People Of Our Redeemer) from Matthew 5:3 —"Blessed are the *poor* in spirit: for theirs is the kingdom of heaven".

Chapter 9

> "And I heard the number of them
> which were sealed: and there were
> sealed an hundred and forty and
> four thousand of all the tribes of
> the children of Israel.
> — *Revelation 7:4*

The Beast smiled as he perused through the battle reports that had been delivered. His forces were doing well, very well, in fact. He was winning campaign after campaign, utilizing the superior knowledge of the Evil One who dwelt within and empowered him. He began to smirk as he read yet another set of reports.

"Not only are we destroying our enemies on the battlefield, but it would seem that we are also wreaking havoc on those so-called 'believers' said Faakhir to Reubens as he poured himself a drink.

"My lord, your plans are ingenious and your strategizing is unparalleled in the annals of human history. Even Alexander the Great would be humbled by your superior thinking abilities" said Reubens.

"I thank you for pointing out the obvious" snickered Faakhir as he sipped his drink. "Tell me, what does our itinerary consist of this week?"

"My lord, you have scheduled a visit to Brussels the day after tomorrow to address the 10 primary full-member leaders of the EU, and then the following day you have a visit from the Pope scheduled" answered Reubens.

Faakhir smiled at the mention of the Pope. He had become quite familiar with him and had used the Pope and the tentacles of his organization to help facilitate his rise to power. But now, he no longer had any need for him.

"Is the Pope presently in Vatican City?" asked Faakhir.

"My lord, I believe that he is. He is not due to leave for two days" answered Reubens.

"Good. Confirm his presence there and then nuke Vatican City" ordered Faakhir nonchalantly.

"My lord, your will be done" replied Reubens as he turned to carry out his orders.

"Oh, and Reubens…"

"Yes, my lord?" answered Reubens.

"Cancel my appointment with the Pope"

said Faakhir, grinning ear-to-ear as he sipped his drink.

Will, Ruby, and the rest of the Body of Christ observed as four angels took standing positions on the four corners of the Earth, not allowing any winds whatsoever to blow on the Earth. Another angel ascended from the east and cried aloud to the four angels whom also were given power to hurt the Earth and the sea, saying "Hurt not the Earth, neither the sea, nor the trees, till we have sealed the servants of our God in their foreheads".

The LORD then summoned Gabriel who immediately appeared before His throne.

"Gabriel, go now, you and your angels, and disperse My sealed servants" commanded the LORD.

"Amen LORD. Thy will be done" replied Gabriel as he then, along with a myriad of other angels, vanished from the Throne Room of Heaven.

Then the Lord Yeshua opened the seventh seal, and such was the intense gravity of the judgments to follow that, immediately, all activity ceased in Heaven and not a single solitary sound was made or heard for the space of half an hour.

The POOR had just finished conducting evening worship when Gabriel and the accompanying angels appeared.

"Blessings upon you from our God" proclaimed Gabriel to all.

"Blessed be the LORD our God" responded John as he approached a little closer to Gabriel, and having just then received a Word of Knowledge added, "Welcome, Gabriel and all who are with you".

"Thank you. The Lord has sealed 144,000 Jews throughout the world to be His faithful servants and to empower and safeguard them for ministry. They will each become as effective and world-reaching as our brother Billy

Graham was during the time of his ministry. Some are here amongst you. We will   transport each servant to his assigned location on the Earth to witness to the populations thereof" informed Gabriel to all.

"The LORD's will be done" replied John, to which everyone nodded in agreement.

"This will not take long" said Gabriel as the angels with him disappeared from sight, and a moment later, so did many members of the POOR, including J. C.

<hr>

Faakhir just could not understand it. It seemed that for every believer that was martyred, three more would rise in his or her place. It was infuriating, and if he didn't have more pressing matters at hand he would have spent more time trying to solve that particular dilemma. However, he had a war to win and a whole world to subjugate, therefore he returned his attention to the situation that was presently before him. The ten full-member state leaders of the EU stood behind him as he spoke to thousands who had jam-packed Wembley Stadium just to hear his voice. Reubens, as always, stood to his right.

"…So I again remind you that we must be as one if we are to bring about our Utopia. Our voices must be as one as well as our actions. We must not allow any dissident voices to try to divide and conquer us. Let no one convince you to serve some Jewish god or His Son, for you yourselves are gods, and I am the god of gods. I, your lord and master, will lead you into the glory of a new world order" said Faakhir, mesmerizing the crowd. He stood silent a moment before continuing. "But, not everyone here is truly with us" he said as he motioned for Reubens and the ten leaders to join him as he stepped down from the dais onto the field. Once on the field, Faakhir separated three of the ten leaders from the group and had them follow him about fifty yards away from the others.

Faakhir then addressed the arena saying "These three are traitors! Their voices and the nations they represent do not "blend" with ours. They are off-key and therefore must be silenced. Reubens…".

Reubens stretched forth his hands towards the heavens and spoke a few dark incantations. Suddenly, from a cloudy sky there fell fiery-red fireballs that completely engulfed the area where the four men stood. The three leaders screamed in agony as they fell to the ground being consumed by the flames, but Faakhir just stood there and watched them burn, totally unaffected in any way. Mere moments later, there remained nothing of the three leaders but ashes, and Faakhir once again addressed the crowd.

"These three are fallen, and so are the traitorous nations they represented. I have conquered them and silenced their dissident voices. I reiterate, no one will stop us from building our heaven here on Earth!" exclaimed Faakhir to the thunderous applause and cheering of the crowd who exulted "Who is like Prince Faakhir?" and "Who can make war against him?"

J.C. found himself back in the U.S., having been instantaneously transported there by an angel after receiving the seal of God in his forehead. He recognized the locale as the suburbs just north of Philadelphia which had not suffered the fate of many other major bicoastal cities.

As he stood looking about, he heard someone call to him.

"Hi, are you J.C.?" asked a middle-aged man walking towards him smiling.

"Yes, I am. Who are you?" replied J.C.

"My name is Manuel Carlos. Call me Manny. The Lord sent me to meet you here. You'll be residing with me, my wife Maria, and our two sons, Manuel Jr. and Miguel" said Manuel as he shook hands with J.C.

"Very nice to meet you Manny. The Lord truly is awesome, isn't he?" said J.C.

"He truly is indeed" replied Manny as he motioned with his hand the direction in which they were to go. "I had just finished my morning devotion when the Lord spoke to me and gave me instructions concerning your mission here. We are honored to be used of the

Lord to bless you".

"Thank you, Manny. May the Lord bless you and your family in return" said J.C.

"He already has, and He will" replied Manny with a knowing wink and smile. "So tell me J.C., where did you learn to speak such fluent Spanish?"

"What are you talking about?" asked J.C. as he stopped in his tracks and looked at Manny, being perplexed. "I'm speaking English. I don't speak Spanish".

Manny grinned from ear-to-ear and exulted "How great is our God! I can't speak anything other than Spanish and yet we both understand what the other is saying. The Lord is just so awesome."

"Amen, brother, amen" said J.C. as they again started on their way to Manny's house, rejoicing in the Lord and praising Him for His mighty works.

All of Heaven watched as seven angels were summoned before the Throne of God and to each of them was given a golden shofar. Then another angel with a golden censer came and stood at the golden altar before the Throne, and there was much incense given to him to be offered with the prayers of the Tribulation saints upon the golden altar. The smoke of the incense, along with the prayers of the saints ascended up before God out of the angel's hand. Then the angel took the censer and filled it with fire from the golden altar and cast it upon the Earth, and there were voices, thunderings and lightnings, and an earthquake. Then the seven angels with the golden shofars prepared themselves to blow.

The first angel blew, and hail and fire mingled with blood appeared, and they were cast upon the Earth.

Thaddeus Worthington IV relaxed on his inflatable floating pool recliner as he listened to a library of his favorite mp3s on his iPod Touch.

"This is the life" he said to no one in particular as he finished what remained of his vodka and orange juice. "Hon", he said to his wife Amanda, lounging poolside, "would you get me another?"

"Honestly Tad, don't you think two is enough, especially this early in the day?" replied Amanda as she rose from her seat to fetch the drink.

"Mandy, please don't start with that again. Can't you just get the drink without all the drama?" he curtly replied as he leaned back and looked at the cloud formations - what few there were.

Their luxurious villa was located just east of Marseille in the south of France on the shore of the Mediterranean and the weather this day was perfect.

Momentarily, Mandy reappeared with Tad's drink and as she began to hand it to him, Tad's eyes grew wide.

"Would you look at that" he exclaimed, his eyes still fixated on the sky.

Amanda turned her attention towards the same and felt a shiver of fear run through her body as she saw what looked like the sky becoming blood-red and filled with fire.

"T-Tad, what's happening?" shrieked Mandy.

"As if I would know!" replied Tad as he hurried to get out of the pool.

As soon as he stood poolside next to Mandy, it began to hail and the two of them ran indoors.

"Man, this is crazy weird" said Tad listening to the incessant barrage of hailstones on his roof and the pavement outside.

"Oh my god, Tad…Tad look at the ground!" exclaimed Mandy.

Tad joined her at the kitchen bay window and peered outside at the ground which was becoming covered with what appeared to be small pockets of blood and flames each time a hailstone would hit it.

"What the …" started Tad.

Suddenly they heard a very loud thump on their roof, followed by ever-more increasingly loud thumps. Then they heard a loud crash outside. As they peered out the window, they saw that their large fiberglass patio table was completely demolished and that the hailstones, which had started out being the size of golf balls, were now the size of basketballs and beach balls which pulverized everything they hit.

"The car!" exclaimed Tad as he ran towards the front door.

"Tad! Are you crazy? Forget the car! Tad! Please! It's too dangerous! Tad!! Tad!!!" screamed Mandy to no avail as Tad ran out the door.

Tad ran towards his prized Bentley, only to see it demolished by a huge hailstone several moments before a large hailstone separated his head from his body.

Mandy, witnessing the demise of her husband, screamed in terror and fainted to the floor.

All over the world, millions of unbelievers poured into hell as death and destruction rained down upon the entire planet, except in Israel and Petra. Multitudes upon multitudes of buildings were outright destroyed or damaged beyond repair. Many farmlands, crops, forests and jungles were burning out of control, as were many tree-lined city neighborhoods. In all, one-third of the trees and all green grass on planet Earth was burning. As a result, mass hysteria and panic gripped many of the survivors of the physical aspect of this plague, and having no sure foundation upon which to stand, they promptly lost their minds.

J.C. along with Manny and his family, watched as the fiery hailstorm raged on. They were quite amazed at the sight, but were even more amazed because Manny's property was not being hit by any hailstones.

"Praise the Lord. This is truly incredible" exclaimed Manny.

The Holy Spirit spoke through J.C. saying "Thus does the Lord your God spare all His servants".

In Israel, as well as in Petra, the skies were clear, while all over the world, believers were miraculously spared from any harm or hurt from the fiery hailstorm, even those caught out in wide open spaces.

"Manny, spread the word. Tomorrow night we'll hold an outreach service at the YMCA" said J.C.

"But we don't know if this will still be going on tomorrow night or not" replied Manny, gesturing towards the sky.

"It will", answered J.C., "but the Lord has revealed to me that anyone that He has drawn to Himself to receive salvation will not be harmed".

"Praise the Lord. His will be done" said Manny as he left to make preparation for the service.

J.C. retired to his room to spend the night in prayerful communion with the Lord.

<u>Chapter 10</u>

…the stars shall fall from heaven,
and the powers of the heavens
shall be shaken - *Matthew 24:29*

Many of the high-ranking members of the Global Astronomers Society (GAS) were meeting in Brussels in emergency session to discuss the matter of the NEOs discovered by the late Dr. Wersop (a member until his recent passing). Knowledge of the existence of Wersop-1 and Wersop-2 was regained after one of Dr. Wersop's closest friends and colleagues finally was able to decipher an encrypted email message that Dr. Wersop had sent to him the day before he died. After many hours of debate, they all came to the same conclusions – that Dr. Wersop's calculations were correct and that it was far too late to attempt to do anything about it now. Now all that remained was the question of whether to notify the general public of the impending impacts. As if the surviving populations of the world didn't have enough to worry about with the planet on fire from nuclear war and fiery hailstorms, they were already beginning to become more and more nervous about the two points of light in the sky which were becoming larger and brighter with each passing day. The GAS members came to the consensus that due to the fact that they weren't absolutely 100% sure as to where the impact points would be, it would be reckless to warn the public and thereby most assuredly creating a worldwide panic which would bring about many premature deaths and needless destruction.

The POOR had just finished their evening worship service when Gabriel appeared before them.

"Shalom" said the mighty angel with a smile.

"Shalom" replied John as he approached humbly.

"I bring you tidings of what will take place

in three days. A huge mountain of rock will fall from the sky and strike your world. It will impact in the sea and many shall be overcome of it, but fear not, for the Lord our God watches over you and the judgment shall not come nigh your dwelling" declared Gabriel.

"The 2nd Trumpet Judgment" said Ant aloud to no one in particular.

"Yes Antwon", said Gabriel as he vanished into the night air, "You are correct...as usual".

Gabriel's last statement made Ant blush and everyone else lovingly giggle. After a few moments of excited chatter, most everyone began to retire for the night and headed towards their domiciles, except for John, Ant, Joey and a few other men.

"Brethren", began John as he addressed the men now present, "Take note of the quicker succession of the Trumpet Judgments as compared to the Seal Judgments, and it is my belief that the Vial or Bowl Judgments will succeed one another even faster".

"I believe that as well" agreed Ant.

"The 'Day of the Lord' is fierce indeed" added Joey as the men sat in a small circle upon rocks.

One of them, a relatively young man named

Justin, asked "I've only been a believer for a very short time and I must admit that there are many things that I don't quite understand. For example, why would God send judgments on the entire Earth, killing not only good men and women, but innocent children as well. I mean, what's the purpose?"

Ant replied "First of all, your logic is flawed because in reality there aren't any "*good*" people and no one is "*innocent*". What the world considers to be good deeds or good works, well, God declares them to be as 'filthy rags'…translated 'soiled sanitary napkins' in the original Greek."

"Again, Ant is correct as usual", chimed in John, drawing a big laugh from the entire group.

When the laughter finally subsided, Justin said "I guess you're right. I never really thought about it that way. Before the Lord saved me, I used to think that at the end of my life, if my 'good' outweighed my 'bad', I would go to Heaven. I'm glad I found out the truth, or rather that the Truth found me."

Everyone joyfully smiled and nodded their heads in agreement as they all said "Amen" in unison.

Joey then replied "What you just said reminds me of how I was able to lead a Muslim acquaintance of mine named Hakeem to the Lord. As you may or may not know, Muslims hold Jesus in very high regard as a true Prophet of Allah, second only to Mohammed himself. Well, Hakeem thought pretty much the same as you did, the whole 'good' vs. 'bad' thing. I asked him if Jesus, being a 'true Prophet' would ever lie. He responded that Jesus would never ever tell a lie. I then asked him that if one gets into Heaven (or Paradise as Hakeem called it) by their 'good' outweighing their 'bad', how is it that Jesus, a 'true Prophet' – who would never lie, tells the malefactor crucified on His right that he would that day be in Paradise with Him. Now mind you, this man is crucified, so he can't do any good works from this point on, and his past is full of sin and crime, hence his execution, which he himself declares to be just. So, if he has no 'good' to outweigh his 'bad' how can Jesus, being a 'true Prophet' - who would never tell a lie, grant to this malefactor a place in Paradise. He could do it because He's who He says He is – the perfect Son of Man, the sinless Son of God, the Lamb of God without blemish who takes away the sin of the world."

"Wow, that's good stuff" said Justin.

"Wow, indeed" said John as the men looked towards the heavens, "Wow, indeed".

———————————————

Heaven resounded with praise to the One who sat on the Throne as the second angel began blowing his trumpet.

———————————————

Wersop-1 screamed westward into the Earth's upper atmosphere over Alaska at three times the speed of sound, creating an earsplitting sonic boom as it did so. It streaked across Earth's sky, burning as if spewed from the very gates of Hell itself, leaving a humongous trail of vapor and smoke as it quickly descended towards its God-ordained destiny. Below, wherever it passed over, panicked spectators by the millions gave a huge sigh of relief and cried, and those still in its path began to wail even louder, fearful of a nearby impact.

However, true to the Holy Scriptures, Wersop-1 impacted in the sea - dead center. It struck with the force of a thousand nuclear detonations, and the noise of the blast was deafening, even on all the surrounding shores of the sea. Immediately, there was a gigantic mushroom cloud consisting of superheated steam, water vapor, and sediment from the ocean floor, as well as a wall of water measuring 1000 ft. high and increasing by the second as the tsunami headed in every direction from the point of impact.

As a result, everything - whether sea-life or sea-faring ships - within the radius of 100 nautical miles from ground zero was totally vaporized, and within the radius between 100 and 500 nautical miles from ground zero, all sea-life was killed and all ships were destroyed along with their crews, turning the sea red with their blood. All told, one-third of all the sea-life and one-third of all the ships in the sea were no more.

J.C., as did the rest of the world, felt the tremor caused by the impact of Wersop-1. He helped Manny calm the rest of the gathered believers as they huddled together in prayer in their underground hideout. They had gone subterranean not so much because of Wersop-1, or 2 for that matter, but rather more due to the demonized, hate-filled persecution of believers, who refused to take the mark of the Beast, and would not refrain from helping any Jews who needed their aid.

"Peace. Peace" said Joey gently over the trembling children, no doubt quieting many adults' fears as well.

J.C. began to sing softly, "When peace like a river attendeth my way, when sorrows like sea billows roll…"

As everyone began to join in, the Spirit of the Lord filled the room where they were and the spirit of fear departed.

J.C. loved this group and his heart went out

to them as they had suffered much loss, for while he knew that no deadly harm could come to him, he also knew firsthand that the same could not be said of them. More than quite a few members had already met with martyrdom, refusing to deny Jesus. Yet, the Lord was faithful and supplied their every need as He deemed it to be, and the group was growing, despite all the persecution - or maybe perhaps in small part because of it.

The world was now truly reeling from the effects of the devastation it had so far endured, and due to the loss of sea-life, famine increased exponentially, and so as well did the number of its fatal victims and many considered them to be the lucky ones - for life itself had become a horror. It seemed that almost everywhere one looked, the scenes and signs of a so-called "normal" life no longer existed. Crime and lawlessness were rampant and appeared to be the order of the day, and supposedly because of this, martial law had now been imposed globally, hence the neighborhoods permeated with military police.

One of these officers, Lt. Robert Crenshaw, now sat in his vehicle outside the house owned and, until recently, inhabited by Manuel Carlos and family. He carefully removed some photographs from a manila envelope and studied them in the light of a miniature flashlight for a short while. Crenshaw then pulled a non-military issue Glock from underneath the glove-box before departing the vehicle under the cover of 2:00 am darkness. He quickly walked to the front door and rang the bell. No answer. He rang the bell a few more times. Still - no answer. He then walked around to the backside of the house, and breaking the glass of the sliding patio door, entered the home.

"Nice place" he said out loud to himself as he gazed at the interior of Manny's house. "Why is it that so many of these traitorous rebels seem to have had such peaceful-looking homes. I don't get it".

Crenshaw carefully and quietly checked each room but found no one to be at home, and judging from the staleness of the air inside, they hadn't been for a while. He then quickly returned to his vehicle and again stared at the photos of Joshua Cohen and Manuel Carlos.

"You can't hide forever. We'll find you yet" said Crenshaw as he drove off into the darkness.

Faakhir bowed himself low to the floor as he gave homage to the Evil One, who now indwelt him and gave him all his power.

"O Lucifer, light of the morning, I implore you, give me the world and I will make it worship you forever. Strike down our enemies, even drag them out of Heaven, so that you alone will rule" prayed Faakhir as the reddish aura that surrounded him deepened even more, visible even in the almost total darkness of the room.

Even though his mouth was now closed, a deep, guttural voice from within Faakhir replied audibly.

"The world is yours for the taking, for I have given it into your hands. You have done well, my son. Together, we will destroy many, including the Elect, so that there will be no reason for the Holy One to return to this planet – and so will it be ours forever. My will be done" hissed Satan.

"Your will be done, my master" said Faakhir as he rose to his feet feeling more empowered.

Faakhir returned to his desk and pressed a button on the console and his flat-panel monitor came to life as Reubens appeared on the screen in response to the live-video call.

"Yes, my lord" inquired Reubens as he straightened his attire.

"You look fine as always, Reubens" smirked Faakhir.

"Thank you sir" replied Reubens feeling a little more at ease.

"Report to my office at once. I have a few things to go over with you that are of vital importance" ordered Faakhir.

"At once, my lord" responded Reubens as he arose from his seat to comply with Faakhir's command.

Faakhir pressed another button and then sat

in his office chair as the screen faded to black again.

J.C., Manny and the other subterranean refugees huddled close together as the cavern they occupied shook from a small temblor caused by a distant nuclear detonation. Incredibly, the warring nations had resumed the insanity that they called WWIII, even after witnessing undeniable judgments from God.

"I…I don't understand. Why would they go back to doing this" asked Manny rather perplexed.

J.C. replied "It's a testament to the darkness that resides in the hearts of mankind. Man *won't* do better because he *can't* do better. He's powerless to do so. Committing sinful acts doesn't make one a sinner. That's putting the proverbial cart before the horse. One commits sinful acts because he is *already* born a sinner. That is the nature of man. He is a slave to sin".

"Thank the Lord that He has set us free from that slavery and darkness" replied Manny smiling.

"'He whom the Son sets free is free indeed'" quoted J.C. to which they all said "Amen".

Someone then said "SSShhhh. I hear voices right above us".

Manny said "I'll go check it out" and began to leave the cavern.

J.C. stopped him in his tracks and said "No, I am commanded to investigate this matter. Help take care of the flock while I am away".

"As the Lord wills" said Manny as he gave J.C. a warm embrace.

J.C. then made his way through the maze of tunnels leading to the entrance of the underground hideout. As he exited the tunnel into the twilight air he sensed the presence of another, and in so turning came face to face with Lt. Crenshaw.

"Hi, I've been looking for you" said Lt. Crenshaw as he began to reach for his sidearm.

"So I've been told, and there's no need for that Lt. Crenshaw – I will come peaceably" replied J.C.

A very discernable look of puzzlement came over Lt. Crenshaw's face as he wondered how in the world could this rebel know who he was.

"So, where's our ride?" asked J.C.

Peals of thunder and lightning emanated from the Throne as the Lord Yeshua commanded the third angel to sound his trumpet. And so he did.

Barely had the inhabitants of the world had time to begin to experience the full effect of the impact from Wersop-1, when Wersop-2 screamed into Earth's upper atmosphere, exuding a trail of radioactive and chemical fallout that seeded the few remaining clouds in the sky, before impacting on mountaintops that were the source of fresh water supplies for many. As a result, one-third of the world's remaining fresh water supply, as scarce as it was, became unusable. And as is usually the case when a vital necessity becomes scarcer and less obtainable, violence and crime increased exponentially, adding to the sky-high and daily escalating death-rate in the world.

Chapter 11

> "The sun shall be turned into darkness,
> and the moon into blood, before the
> great and terrible day of the Lord come."
> *- Joel 2:31*

It was daybreak in Petra with the sun rising over the horizon as Ant descended a small hill where he spent the early pre-dawn hours in prayer and meditation with the Lord. He entered his "home" and greeted Miriam with a kiss and placed his hand on her belly. Miriam was with child and they were elated. As they did not have any advanced medical technology there in Petra, they did not know whether they were having a boy or a girl, which only added to the excitement of all.

"So have you guys decided on any names at all" asked Joey who entered from the other "suite".

"Actually, we have. If it's a boy – "Joshua" and if it's a girl – "Esther" replied Miriam glowingly.

"Those are great biblical names. Nice. And to think, that the child will actually get to meet their ancient namesake in person and talk with them. That is just so awesome. God is so great" said Joey very excitedly.

Everyone agreed, including Sarah who had just joined them, as they all sat down to breakfast and holding hands, gave thanks unto the Lord.

Manny and his family, along with the other refugees, prayed for J.C. as well as others during their evening worship service conducted in their underground "home". Although everyone was concerned about J.C., the worship was Spirit-filled.

Lt. Crenshaw had never experienced

anything like this before in all his days of law enforcement. He had never encountered a fugitive that was more at peace than he was himself. One who seemed to be sincerely more concerned about how *he* was coping, rather than the fugitive's own predicament. Now that they had reached the station, he hoped that being in familiar surroundings would help him regain control of the situation. It did not.

"I want to know why you and the others in your factions are going around fomenting rebellion and treason" demanded Lt. Crenshaw.

"It is not rebellion or treason to serve the one true King of Kings and Lord of Lords" offered J.C.

'There can only be one Lord" said Crenshaw.

"True, and Faakhir ain't it" answered J.C.

"You'll recant those words before you die" threatened Crenshaw, his face red with anger.

"Actually, I'll be singing them as I leave this place when my work here at this prison is done" said J.C., smiling as he was led to his waiting cell block.

The Lord Yeshua commanded the fourth angel to sound his trumpet. And so he did.

The Earth was a desolation, the result of human insanity and divine judgments. As a result of all the explosive impacts, whether nuclear, cosmic, or divine, the Earth's upper atmosphere was permeated with a thick haze which covered the entire planet. So thick was this blanket of dust, dirt and ash that the amount of light that would normally reach the Earth, whether from the sun, or the stars, or reflected by the moon, was reduced by one-third. During the middle of the day it seemed like twilight, and in the middle of the night it was extremely dark and more fear further gripped the hearts of them that dwelt upon the Earth, whose names were not written in the Lamb's Book of Life from the beginning of the ages.

Lt. Crenshaw was at the end of his rope. He did not know what to do about the rebel J.C. who was leading many of the prisoners to faith in Jesus Christ. He couldn't kill him because the High Command wanted to interrogate J.C. themselves, and he was beginning to believe that he probably couldn't kill him even if he tried because no matter how badly they beat him after he would lead another soul to Christ, his wounds would be completely healed by the next day as if he had never been touched, which would only serve to give credence to his message, thereby leading to the saving of even more souls. He couldn't let him go because that would be the end of his career, possibly his life, and he knew that J.C. wouldn't try to break out of prison so he couldn't say that J.C. was killed during an attempted prison break. Crenshaw wiped the sweat from his brow as he listened to J.C. and the new "believers" sing unto their Lord. Crenshaw looked at the clock. Midnight.

Unable to bear anymore, he marched into their cell block, determined at least to put a stop to this, when suddenly an overpowering bright light momentarily blinded him. As his eyes adjusted slightly to the brilliant dazzling light, he could see that the light emanated from what vaguely appeared to be the form of a man. Crenshaw could not move a muscle, so overpowering was the spectacle. He then observed the being lifting what appeared to be a sword and striking the cell block floor with it. Immediately the entire building began to shake as well as the ground beneath it. As a result, all the cell doors were opened, but the only ones able to walk in the light were the believers who very quickly escaped, except for J.C., who very calmly walked up to the momentarily paralytic Lt. Crenshaw as he sang "Our God is an Awesome God", smiled and disappeared into the night.

The Body of Christ, seated before the Throne, listened and watched as the Lord Yeshua gave a brass key to Michael and a message to Gabriel and sent them on their way.

Gabriel, having reached his destination in the midst of the heavens, began to cry aloud "Woe, woe, woe to the inhabiters of the Earth by reason of the other voices of the trumpet of the three angels, which are yet to sound". His message was heard and understood by every human being on the face of the Earth regardless of language, tongue, dialect, or degree of hearing disability.

The Lord Yeshua then commanded the fifth angel to sound his trumpet. And so he did.

Michael, on the other hand, traveled all the way to the Earth where, in the spirit realm, he delivered the brass key into the slithery hands of the demon Apollyon, and then promptly returned to Heaven.

Apollyon immediately used the brass key to open the bottomless pit from which poured forth countless demonic beings and so much smoke that it further darkened the sun and the air. They were commanded by the Lord not to hurt any green thing but to only hurt those who did not have the seal of God in their foreheads. They were also commanded not to kill them but to torment them with a sting like as that of a scorpion. And torment them they did. So much so that people everywhere sought to take their own lives, but found to their horror that Death fled from them, so not only did they suffer from the demonic stings, but also from the normally deadly wounds they inflicted upon themselves. What hospitals there were remaining were overflowing with people with such horrific self-inflicted injuries that the medical staffs were completely terrified because they knew that there was no way that people in such states should still be alive. This demonic attack would bring woe and misery for five months, and there were yet two woes more to come.

Faakhir's Imperial Palace was unraveling into a shamble, as was, many would say, his worldwide Empire. The five months of unbearable torment had so incapacitated his government that everything had come to a complete standstill. Even the war, which the last time he had checked he was winning, more or less ground to a halt, thanks to a truce necessitated by the worldwide demonic attacks.

Faakhir summoned Ruebens to his office. Ruebens arrived promptly as usual and stood before Faakhir's desk.

"Have a seat Reubens" directed Faakhir as he leaned back in his executive leather chair. "I want to share with you some things that are about to transpire. Even as I speak, the armies of the kings of the East are gathering together to prepare to march on us here at Babylon, as are the armies of the king of the South. They believe that they can destroy me. Not so, but I have another purpose for us all to be gathered together – to march on Israel and forever destroy the Jews and Jerusalem".

"Your Majesty, please forgive your humble servant's ignorance, but why the great hatred of the Jews and the city of Jerusalem?" asked Reubens tepidly.

"Because He loves them and has promised them a Kingdom encompassing this entire world which He would rule from Jerusalem. Are you forgetting that it was they that He chose to bring forth the Messiah, the Savior? This world is mine and when I destroy the Jews and Jerusalem, He will have no reason to return to it. That is why we have tried to exterminate the Jews time and again, but this time, we will not fail" replied Faakhir.

"But sir, isn't that what was said all the other times, and begging your Majesty's pardon, sir, isn't your current plan exactly what is supposed to bring Him back – to save His people from extinction" asked Ruebens.

Faakhir slowly stood up as he gave Ruebens an icy stare, saying between clenched teeth "I think you've been reading too many fairytales. Besides, even if He dared to show up, I'll have all the armies of the world train their trigger-hairs on Him. This is my world now and no one is going to wrest it away from me, not even Him. Are we clear?"

"Yes sir", replied Reubens. "Crystal".

The Lord commanded the sixth angel to sound and so he did.

Chapter 12

> "By these three were the third part of men killed, by the fire, and by the smoke, and by the brimstone, which issued out of their mouths."
>
> *- Revelation 9:18*

Faakhir was wrapping up the end of a long and acerbic scolding being given to the Israeli PM as they exited the PM's office.

"Accompany me to the Temple Mount. We'll see what can be done about those two agitators" he said gruffly to the PM.

"Yes sir, I'm right with you" replied the PM, nervously joining in step with Faakhir as they strode towards the foyer of the Knesset.

Minutes later they arrived at the top of the Temple Mount and came within several yards of the Two Witnesses.

The Two Witnesses addressed the Israeli PM saying in perfect unison "For forty and two months we have preached the gospel of the Kingdom and shown with many great signs and wonders that Yeshua is the Christ, yet still you have hardened your heart against the Word of the Lord, therefore your house is left to you desolate and this day you shall reap what you have sown".

"W-What do you mean by that?" asked the PM.

They both answered him, again in perfect unison, saying "It shall be revealed to you shortly, but as for us, our mission is now at its end and the appointed hour of our departure is at hand".

"You are so right about that" yelled Faakhir as he pulled his Baby Desert Eagle from inside his jacket and fired two shots, each finding their mark. The Two Witnesses both slumped to the ground motionless. Faakhir then walked over to them and emptied his clip into their bodies, looking up at the PM saying "Just to be sure" with a sinister smile on his face as he then reloaded his weapon.

The PM, his mouth hanging open yet unable to speak, looked on in total shock.

Faakhir, then stepping over the bodies of the Two Witnesses, commanded that their bodies not be touched and proceeded to walk up the steps leading to the Temple entrance with gun in hand, past the Court of the Gentiles, past the

Soreq, past the Court of the Women, past the Court of the Israelites, and into the Court of the Priests where he was confronted by the High Priest.

"How dare you enter the holy courts! You shall die!" exclaimed the High Priest.

Faakhir replied "I already have" and shot the High Priest right between the eyes.

The other priests scattered as Faakhir made his way past the Holy Place into the Holy of Holies.

Once inside, he sat upon the newly erected Throne of David situated in the exact center of the room, and with all the regal-bearing he could muster he loudly declared "I am the Lord, your God!"

Upon seeing and hearing this, the remaining priests tore their garments and screamed out "Blasphemy, Blasphemy" as they ran from the Temple.

As news of this spread, all the believers in Judea suddenly began fleeing to Petra. However, a little more than two-thirds of the Jews remained in Israel.

The Israeli PM, having witnessed all, crumpled to the floor of the Temple in complete and utter shock. As he lay there, the words of the Two Witnesses seemed to echo in the Temple, and his heart, which had been beating wildly, just simply stopped.

Ant was standing atop one of the high ridges in Petra along with Joey, John and a few of the other leaders when he noticed what seemed to be a small dust-storm kicking up far away over in the area towards Israel.

"Here they come!" said Ant, drawing everyone's attention to what he was seeing.

"Hallelujah" exclaimed John. "Let's go down and greet them as they arrive.

"We'd better hurry. Whatever mode of transportation they're using to get here, they're moving awfully fast" observed Joey.

They quickly descended to ground level and headed to Petra's entrance.

The fleeing refugees from Israel numbered roughly more than two million, but they moved as one. It was a surreal sight to behold. They moved effortlessly across the desert highway. It seemed almost as if they were gliding along the surface. They practically were. Unseen by the human eye, more than a million angels were escorting the refugees – one in each hand. Even the refugees were unaware of their presence. All they knew was that their running was mysteriously effortless and easy. No one was becoming tired and no one wanted to stop until they reached Petra.

Faakhir summoned Mark Reubens, as well as his local commanders, to the Holy of Holies where he sat. As they approached the throne they bowed before him. Faakhir gestured for the False Prophet to come closer and he obeyed.

"I do not wish to be constrained to remain in this one place at all times, but I do want everyone to recognize that this is my temple and that my presence will always be here. Therefore, I want a statue of my likeness, made of the purest gold, to be erected here so that all may continue to worship me, even in my absence" ordered Faakhir.

"My Lord, I have already anticipated your desire. The statue is prepared. Your will be done" replied Reubens as he bowed and backed out from the room.

"Very good" said Faakhir, somewhat impressed. "As for the rest of you", "Many Judeans have fled into the wilderness towards Jordan. I want you to catch them and slaughter them. I want no survivors. Understood?"

"Yes, my Lord" replied the commanders as they too bowed, backed their way out of the room and rushed out - each to their own platoons.

As the last of the fleeing refugees entered into Petra, a lookout stationed on one of the high ridges radioed down to one of the leaders and informed him that he was observing what appeared to be a humongous dust cloud forming in the far distance towards Israel.

"More than likely, that would be the "flood" sent to pursue the remnant of God's people" offered Ant.

"Let's go up onto one of the high ridges so we can witness the deliverance and protection of the Lord" suggested Joey.

The rest of the leaders agreed and took to higher ground, as did many other onlookers. There were many Jews present who had not yet trusted in Yeshua as Messiah, but had also fled at the urging of the others, so John, at the leading of the Spirit, took advantage of the moment and addressed them. He did not yell or shout, but his voice was heard and understood by all, even those of other tongues.

"I now speak to my brethren, who as yet have not believed in Yeshua as Messiah. I tell you now that the things you have witnessed this day were foretold 2,000 years ago by my namesake John who recorded the visions given to him by Yeshua the Messiah in the book of The Revelation. You are blessed in that you are about to witness another prophecy from that same book come true. It was prophesized that when you saw the 'abomination that makes desolate stand in the Holy Place' that you would flee to this place, and here you stand. It was also prophesized that Satan, through his Antichrist, would send a 'flood' of troops to pursue you and destroy you, but that the Lord would cause the Earth to help you by opening its mouth and swallowing them up. Well, they're on their way and we would be defenseless except that the Lord, our God fights for us. You will be eyewitnesses to the truth and veracity of the New Testament Scriptures, and above all, you will know that Yeshua is Lord" proclaimed John. "Behold, I have told you beforehand, so that when it comes to pass, you will know the words I speak are true".

As John finished speaking, everyone noticed that the light over the desert began to diminish ever so gradually. It seemed to be the same ambience as whenever there would be a partial eclipse of the sun but the mid-afternoon sun was shining brightly and there was hardly a cloud in the sky.

The throngs in Heaven were ecstatic and filled with anticipation as the Father spoke.

"Michael, it is the time", instructed the LORD.

"Amen, LORD", answered Michael as he stood up from his seat near the throne and then vanished from sight.

The POOR watched as the Antichrist's troops advanced closer and closer. They were nearly within three miles of Petra when, unseen by all, Michael alighted in the midst of the enemy troops. He then lifted his mighty sword and struck the Earth. Immediately there was a ferociously violent earthquake and a huge chasm opened up as the ground gave way and the entire host of pursuing troops fell down alive into hell with their screams and yelling blending in with the wails and moans emanating from below. Michael then struck the

Earth again and the chasm closed up as the desert was made level once again.

In the desert – deathly silence. In Petra – praise and worship was going up to the Lord as never before by everyone, including those who previously hadn't acknowledged Yeshua as Messiah. There were no doubts in their hearts now as they also placed their trust in Yeshua as Lord and Messiah.

A few days later on the Temple Mount, Faakhir stood defiantly before the Temple as he spoke to the world via a hastily convened news conference. Several yards away the bodies of the Two Witnesses still lay undisturbed where they fell nearly four days ago.

"My brothers and sisters, I join with you in your celebration of the deliverance that my own hands have wrought on your behalf. Today I present you with a gift from your Lord. Reubens…" said he as he turned towards the

False Prophet, who was standing next to something tall and veiled. As Reubens unveiled a huge statue made in the exact image and likeness of Faakhir, he began to speak dark incantations over it. Suddenly, the statue became lifelike and it began to speak.

"At the sound of my voice, whenever you shall hear it, all will bow and give worship to me. Whosoever will not bow and worship me, shall die. Everyone will receive a mark of loyalty in their right hand as a sign of submission to my rule. Amputees and paralytics will receive the mark in their foreheads. Whosoever will not receive the mark of loyalty will not be able to buy, sell, or engage in any kind of commerce whatsoever. It has been decreed, so let it be done!"

Upon hearing this, the crowds of people present went to their knees and began to worship the image of the Beast. This went on for about four minutes until there was heard some screaming and a great commotion following. All eyes turned to where the Two Witnesses lay. Almost everyone was scared out of their wits as the Two Witnesses stood upon their feet. Their countenance was even brighter than before as they now possessed glorified bodies. Then they heard a Voice from Heaven command **"Come up here"**. Millions worldwide watched as the Two Witnesses rose up through the clouds to Heaven, and there was none that could deny what they saw. As the onlookers stood gazing into the sky, the earth began shaking around them as Jerusalem was hit by a massive earthquake which, by the time it was all over, would claim over seven thousand lives.

The Chinese Premiere made one phone call after concluding his video conference with his fellow accomplice from the North.

"Mobilize" he simply commanded the person on the other end of the line.

At this one word command more than 200 million men, troops from among all the Kings of the East, began the long march on Jerusalem to join with the armies of the North and the South to make war against the Beast.

The POOR were concluding their daily twilight worship service when Arizael yet again appeared before them.

"Shalom. Peace be unto you" said Arizael greeting all.

"Hello Arizael" replied Ant as he stood upon his feet.

"Hello Ant. Just so you know, Ant, your rendition of 'How Great Thou Art' sounds just as "good" as your 'Livin' For The City', but He insists that it still blesses Him so" said Arizael smiling.

"Thanks – I think" replied Ant sheepishly as everyone around him shared a good chuckle.

"Hello Arizael. To what do we owe the honor of your presence this evening" inquired John.

"To the contrary, it is I who am honored to come before you, fellow brethren of the Lord" replied Arizael. "As you are well aware, this land will soon be covered with troops from every nation. As you are also aware, one cannot serve in the military unless they have received the mark of the Beast, therefore every one of them are damned to spend eternity in the Lake of Fire. However, there are still many Jews in Israel who have not taken the mark who will need to be led here. Of a truth, not all will come - for the Scripture must come to pass that two-thirds of all Israel will be cut off, but the Lord will bring the third through the fire and both save and sanctify them. Send seventy men, full of the Holy Spirit, to lead these remaining stragglers back here to safety. The Lord will lead and guide the seventy as to where to go and what to do."

"The will of the Lord be done" replied John.

"Shalom and good night to all" said Arizael as he vanished from sight.

John immediately went into prayer to seek the counsel of the Lord as to whom he should send. It took only a few minutes as the Lord directed John whom to select. John selected Ant, Joey, and four other men named David, Aaron, Paul, and Matthew, plus sixty-four others. He gathered them all together for prayer, laid hands on each of them, and sent them on their way two-by-two.

Sarah and Miriam, along with the families of the other men, watched with bated breath as their men left the supernaturally safe confines of Petra and headed in the direction of Israel, wondering if they would see them again this side of heaven.

John, sensing their apprehensions, reassured them. "Don't fret dear ones, neither let fear overtake you. They are eternally safe in the bosom of our Lord and you shall see them again. In the meantime, let us pray for their success in doing the Lord's will".

Having been encouraged by John's gracious words, the families came together and prayed, and the peace of God filled their hearts to rejoicing.

The Russian Premier finished watching the video of the Temple Mount happenings and turned from his monitor to address his colleagues who had joined him for a meeting of their "coalition of nations".

"As you can see, this Faakhir cannot be 'Almighty' or else he would not have allowed those two so-called prophets to arise from the dead nor to escape from his hand. No, I'm convinced that what we are dealing with here is a shrewd and very deadly megalomaniac, but he's not invincible. He has maneuvered his way into controlling almost the entire Earth through his deceit, but he will not control us. We will come against him like a whirlwind and drive him into the sea. We will attack him on three fronts. You, the African coalition, will strike first, attacking him from the south. Then we the Russian coalition, while his forces are engaged in battle with you, will strike at him from the north. Finally, the troops from the east, who are mobilizing as we speak, will attack on the eastern front. He will not be able to stand against us all, and so shall he fall" he said matter-of-factly.

The Egyptian President asked him "When do you want us to strike?"

"In ten days at exactly 02:00 hrs their time you will fire the first cruise missile. Remember, no one is to use any nukes, tactical or otherwise. Is that understood?" replied the

Russian Premier.

Everyone nodded and answered in the affirmative.

"Good. Now let us all return to our command posts and use the remaining hours to map out our deployment strategies. Good hunting, comrades", said the Premier as he ended the meeting.

Ten days later, after the POOR had settled down for the night, 'round midnight Arizael appeared to John and several others who were in prayer.

"Blessings upon you all" said Arizael as he greeted those present.

"So what tidings bring you to us this night" asked John solemnly.

"Two hours from now the king of the south will attack the Beast, followed by an attack from the king of the north as well, not to mention the approach of the hordes from the kings of the east. It will be the beginning of the end of Gentile rule in the Earth. It shall eventually involve and affect the entire earth and shall not end until Yeshua returns and destroys the armies at Armegeddon. It shall not, however, come nigh your dwelling for the Lord your God protects you. He has assigned Michael, the great prince, to guard you and to compass you about with the hosts of Heaven, for you are all well beloved. Shalom" said Arizael with great affection.

Upon hearing this, the believers began to praise and worship the Lord with hearts filled with thankfulness and humble adoration.

The air was filled with the sounds of mortar and gunfire as Ant and Joey stealthily neared their assigned destination in east Jerusalem as the city was now under siege by invading troops.

"Remind me if we get back…" started Ant.

"When we get back" corrected Joey.

"Okay – when we get back – to ask Arizael why they couldn't have done this. I mean, it would have taken them all of ten seconds to whisk the stragglers back to Petra." said Ant.

"I'm not sure, but I think it's possibly a matter of faith" replied Joey.

"What do you mean?" said Ant.

"Well if you remember, the first group that fled to Petra was already on its way when the angels began to help them, so their hearts were already fixed and their decisions made by faith, whereas, if the angels were to intercede here, it would not be a matter of faith, but sight. So by sending us humans, the people have to make up their minds and trust in their hearts that what we tell them is true. In other words, they have to take it on faith" replied Joey.

"Riiiiight. That makes sense. Not that I was actually going to question Arizael about anything!" said Ant with a quiet laugh.

They finally reached what appeared to be an abandoned burnt-out factory building.

"I believe this is it" said Joey as Ant nodded in agreement as they began to enter.

The two men quietly walked through the debris strewn about the floor as they made their way towards the rear of the building as the night sky occasionally lit up with weapons fire.

They soon found what they were searching for – a large metal door in the floor which covered the entrance to the lower levels below. They pulled on the door handle. Locked. From the other side.

Ant knelt down next to the door and knocked three times, paused, then knocked seven times, paused, then knocked a final three times.

There was a commotion down below and finally a voice whispering "Who's there"?

Joey answered "Lift up your heads, O you gates…and the King of glory shall come in".

The voice replied "Who is this King of glory"?

Ant answered "The Lord of Hosts, He is the King of glory".

At this, the door was unlocked and began to slowly rise from the floor. A middle-aged man standing on the ladder leading up to the door peered at the two strangers standing above him and asked "Who are you, and how did you know our secret knock and our authentication saying"?

Ant replied "We just did as the Lord God instructed us to do, that's all".

At this, the wary man's eyes brightened as he told them to come down and lock the door behind them and then turned and descended the ladder.

As Ant and Joey reached the lower level, the man introduced himself to them.

"My name is Menachem" he said, then adding "And you are…?

Joey answered him saying "My name is Joseph and my friend is named Antwon, but you can call us Joey and Ant, for short. We are here on a mission given directly by God".

"Please, please come" urged Menachem as he began walking down a dimly lit corridor that seemingly led to nowhere.

As they came to a certain point in the long hallway, Menachem came to a stop and knocked hard against what appeared to be just another part of the corridor's wall, but when he did so, an extremely heavy and perfectly blending door began to open into the hallway.

Menachem entered and motioned for the guys to follow him in, which they did. Once on the other side of the door, the three men required to push the door open due to the taut heavy-duty spring apparatus attached to the door began to allow the door to close slowly, so as to not allow it to slam shut, as it would most certainly do if not for their measured resistance.

"Please, follow me" said Menachem as he began to walk through several rooms until they reached a stairwell that led down to even lower levels.

"I'm beginnin' to feel like Alice going down the rabbit hole" quipped Ant to Joey.

"I know what you mean" replied Joey.

Menachem chuckled and said "Good one. You two are funny".

They all shared a laugh as they began descending the stairwell down two levels. As Menachem led them down the hallway they came to a room which contained several flat panel monitors and three men who were monitoring them. Ant noticed that some of the images on the screens came from the outside of the factory building via tiny hidden cameras.

"Gentlemen, may I present Ant and Joey" said Menachem to the three men in the room.

The three men warmly responded hello, but did not take their eyes off the screens.

"We will be in the Meeting Room" Menachem informed the three men as he, Ant and Joey turned and left the room.

Upon entering the Meeting Room, Ant and Joey were met by several men who stood to their feet at their arrival.

Menachem introduced everyone present and then turned to Ant and Joey.

"We are here in the Meeting Room because I had a dream in which the Lord God said that He was going to send us a message at this hour and to take heed that we obey it. So speak, ye messengers of God" implored Menachem.

"Glory to God! We will speak, but we must speak to all. Will you please convene everyone in this room, including the men you have in the monitoring room. All must hear" said Joey.

"But they must watch…" started Menachem.

"The Lord God and His angels will watch over us" assured Ant.

"Okay, it'll be done" complied Menachem, a little hesitantly.

Two hours later, Ant and Joey were finishing their message to the people. There wasn't a dry eye in the place as the people realized that the One they had denied for so long was the Holy One of Israel who loved them so and gave His life for them. They all repented and gave their hearts, lives, and wills to Him.

Menachem asked "So what do we need to bring along with us?"

"Just yourselves. The Lord has provided all that you need at Petra" answered Ant.

"Let's just get moving and don't be afraid of the sounds of war" added Joey.

At that, Ant and Joey led the people out of the edifice and, eventually, out of the city towards Petra.

"Just keep heading in that direction toward Petra' instructed Ant to Menachem and his group.

"Where are you two going" asked Menachem as he noticed Ant and Joey beginning to fall back towards Jerusalem.

"We have more people to help rescue" answered Joey.

"Oh, okay. Well, thank you and God be with you. Shalom" said Menachem.

"He is, and He's also with you" replied Ant as they parted ways.

Menachem and his group turned towards Petra and began walking quickly. Before they knew it, they were nearly flying towards Petra, being carried along by the angels of God.

The Beast gloried in victory after victory over all his enemies. The king of the south had come against him and he responded so swiftly and so mercilessly that their first encounter was over almost before it began. He struck like lightning, gloriously destroying all in his path. So swift was his victory that when the king of the north came against him, there was no other front that he had to be concerned with, as had been the plan of the king of the north. So he was able to bring all his forces to bear against the northern king and his army. Again his victory was overwhelming and swift. Having won these first two battles, he nevertheless knew that the war would be far from over. He therefore planted his Command Post in Israel, near the border of Iraq.

While the major conflicts took place in Eurasia, the whole world was engulfed in the horrors and chaos resulting from the war. As a result of this war one-third of all remaining humankind would be killed. Over the next three years all the nations' remaining nuclear weapons would be used against each other, resulting in a burnt Earth with very few men left upon it. Even so, men would not turn from their evil, but rather continued to blaspheme the name of God in Heaven.

<u>Epilogue</u>

> "The nations were angry,
> and Your wrath has come,
> And the time of the dead,
> that they should be judged."
> -   *Rev. 11:18*

Heaven was abuzz as the seventh angel stood at the ready before the Throne of God awaiting the Lord's command.

"Sound" commanded the Lord.

The angel sounded his trumpet and immediately there were loud voices in Heaven, saying, "The kingdoms of this world have become the kingdoms of our Lord and of His Christ, and He shall reign forever and ever!"

At this, the Body of Christ, now enthroned before the Throne of God, fell on their faces and worshiped the Lord God.

Will Jackson, among the glorified saints as they resumed their seats, wondered in his heart about his son Antwon's well-being.

The Lord graciously spoke to Will's heart

letting him know that Ant was now one of His own and fulfilling the Lord's purposes for his life.

Knowing this, Will now looked forward to being reunited with his son in the Kingdom, which he knew would soon be made manifest in the Earth. However, he also knew that before that happened, the Earth and its inhabitants would have to endure the remaining seven last plagues to be sent from the Throne of God as He finishes pouring out His wrath on a rebellious, Christ-rejecting world. As bad as things were in the Earth, they would quickly get a whole lot worse before they would get better.

"Even so, Thy will be done, O Lord" said Will in his heart.

The Lord, Who sees, hears and knows all, smiled and spoke to Will's heart, "My will shall be done, my good and faithful servant".

Winter 2010